# CILLA
# LEE-JENKINS

Future Author
Extraordinaire

CILLA LEE-JENKINS

*Future Author* *Extraordinaire*

BY SUSAN TAN

ILLUSTRATED BY DANA WULFEKOTTE

Roaring Brook Press
New York

Published by Roaring Brook Press
Roaring Brook Press is a division of Holtzbrinck Publishing Holdings
Limited Partnership
175 Fifth Avenue, New York, New York 10010

mackids.com

Library of Congress Cataloging-in-Publication Data

Names: Tan, Susan, author. | Wulfekotte, Dana, illustrator.
Title: Cilla Lee-Jenkins: future author extraordinaire / Susan Tan ;
    illustrated by Dana Wulfekotte.
Description: First edition. | New York : Roaring Brook Press, 2017. |
    Summary: "A half-Chinese, half-Caucasian girl's 'memoir'
    about a new sibling, being biracial, and her path to literary
    greatness"—Provided by publisher.
Identifiers: LCCN 2016009081 (print) | LCCN 2016036034
    (ebook) | ISBN 9781626725515 (hardback) | ISBN
    9781626725522 (Ebook)
Subjects: | CYAC: Family life—Fiction. | Friendship—Fiction. |
    Authorship—Fiction. | Chinese Americans—Fiction. | Racially
    mixed people—Fiction. | BISAC: JUVENILE FICTION / Social
    Issues / Friendship. | JUVENILE FICTION / Humorous Stories. |
    JUVENILE FICTION / Girls & Women. | JUVENILE FICTION /
    People & Places / United States / Asian American.
Classification: LCC PZ7.1.T37 Ci 2017 (print) | LCC PZ7.1.T37
    (ebook) | DDC [Fic]—dc23
LC record available at https://lccn.loc.gov/2016009081

Our books may be purchased in bulk for promotional, educational,
or business use. Please contact your local bookseller or the Macmillan
Corporate and Premium Sales Department at (800) 221-7945 ext. 5442
or by e-mail at MacmillanSpecialMarkets@macmillan.com.

First edition, 2017
Book design by Andrew Arnold
Printed in the United States of America by LSC Communications US,
LLC (Lakeside Classic), Harrisonburg, Virginia

1   3   5   7   9   10   8   6   4   2

*For sisters*
*Priscilla & Gwendolyn*
*Catherine & Sarah*

# A (VERY IMPORTANT) LETTER FROM THE AUTHOR

**Dear Reader,**

Before I tell you my story, we need to talk about time machines.

Specifically, I was hoping you might have one.

And if you do, I have a BIG favor to ask.

My name is Priscilla Lee-Jenkins, and I'm destined for greatness as a future author extraordinaire. My only problem is that Priscilla is a TERRIBLE name, and have you ever seen a book with a Lee-Jenkins on the cover? I didn't think so.

So, I need someone with a time machine to travel back eight and a half years, to the day I was born, and make sure I get a name that'll grab people's attention. Like Ruby, because it's pretty. Or Claudia, because it's cool. Or Supernova, because supernovas are bright and shiny and big. I also need ONE last name. Something like Smith or Lilac or Hemingway.

I can tell you exactly where to aim your time machines. I was born at 12:04 a.m. on a holiday called Labor Day. My mom says this is just like me, with a "real literal streak." She says this means I take things at face value, though I don't quite understand, because I don't think values can have faces.

*Anyway,* my point is that holidays are easy to find in the calendar, so getting to the night I was born won't be hard. But then comes the tricky part. You have to steal my birth certificate and change my name without anyone in my family seeing. This will be hard, because the night I was born was Very Unusual, and not just because I was coming into the world ready for a life of literary greatness. The night I was born is also the *only* time my whole family (me, my mom and dad, my Grandma and Grandpa Jenkins, and my Nai Nai and Ye Ye, which are Chinese for "Grandmother" and "Grandfather") has EVER been together in the same room.

So be careful. That's A LOT of people to look out for.

You'll have to be extra sneaky.

You'll also have to be fast, because the baby in my mom's stomach is already getting kind of big. It's going to be normal and boring, not destined for greatness like me, which is one of the (many) reasons I've decided I won't like it. My parents say it's okay to be nervous, and my Grandma and Grandpa Jenkins gave me this journal because they say writing about it will help me understand my feelings.

But I *already* understand my feelings. I don't want to be a Big Sister. I like my family the way it is now. And my best friend Colleen says that when new babies come, they're all the adults want to talk about. Also, she says that they come with things called Responsibilities, which means I'll have to be quiet when the baby is sleeping, and only hold it when I'm sitting on the couch with a pillow under me. Colleen has two little brothers, which means she's been through this A LOT, and it doesn't sound fun *at all*.

So I've decided to take action.

I'm going to write my first-ever book right here in this journal, and I'm going to become a famous bestselling author (with an EXCELLENT new name) before the baby is born. Then no one can forget about me. Also, maybe then my parents will let me name the baby, which they say is Not Going to Happen.

4

My dad once told me that authors should write what they know, but that seemed like *terrible* advice because I've never known a dragon, and dragons are some of the most exciting things you can write about. But now that I need to write my book before the baby gets here, I can see his point. Most of the best stories I know are about things that have happened to me. So this story will be about the thing I know best. Me, Priscilla Lee-Jenkins.

I'm very excited to write the story of my life. It's a GREAT story, with EXCELLENT characters and Struggles and Plot Twists. Also, there's lots of drama. So I think my book will definitely be a bestseller. Plus, you'll get to hear all about my destiny as a future author (and how it makes me *much* better than a new baby), which means that once I'm famous, you'll already know who the real Priscilla (or Claudia or Roswitha or Sparkledust) was as a child.

I'd kind of hoped that before I even finished this letter, some time-traveling reader would've already taken action, and I'd suddenly realize that my name is something AMAZING like Supernova Hemingway.

But I think I'm still Priscilla, which means it hasn't worked yet.

So while I wait, I've resigned myself to Cilla for short, and I'll start my story as:

Your friend,

And maybe new favorite author,

# CILLA LEE-JENKINS
Future Author Extraordinaire

P.S. Isn't that a great word, "resigned"? It means you've given up, but with dignity, and only after a Long and Tortuous Struggle. There are LOTS of Long and Tortuous

Struggles in a world that lets parents name their child Priscilla Lee-Jenkins. Also in a world that insists flying pigs aren't real (they're out there somewhere, I know it—probably hiding with all the people with time machines).

# FAMILIES AND THE
# FORCES OF DARKNESS

**I'll start by introducing my family, since lots of** my stories have them in it (also they're pretty great). There's me (who you know), and my mom and dad. Then there are my mom's parents, my Grandma and Grandpa Jenkins. They live in a big house with black shutters, on top of a tall hill that's fun to roll down. I see them most Saturday mornings for brunch, and Thursdays when Grandpa Jenkins picks me up from school because my parents have to work late. I like Thursdays. Grandpa Jenkins takes me to the park, and sometimes we get hot fudge sundaes. But we don't tell my parents, or Grandma Jenkins.

My dad's parents, my Nai Nai and Ye Ye, also

live very close to us. They live in an apartment in a tall brick building, and I see them every Wednesday, which is the night my parents go out to dinner. On Wednesdays, my Nai Nai picks me up from school, and we go shopping in Chinatown. I love Chinatown. There are so many good smells and new foods there, and my Nai Nai's friends always pat my cheek and give me candy. Plus, the grocery store owner keeps a jar at the counter with two tiny turtles inside, who I've named Green Eggs and Ham, and who I'll take home as pets someday, I've decided.

I love my family just the way they are *now*, with no new baby to get in the way.

In fact, when I told my mom this morning at breakfast that I was writing my book, I said that not wanting a new baby was going to be a BIG theme. And themes are things that happen again and again, like when you put your fingers through the small holes in the fence outside and they get stuck. Then your mom has to use soap to get them out, and she says, "Why did you do that? This happens every time!" Which means if something's a theme, it happens A LOT.

## MY FAMILY TREE

My mom liked the idea of my book so much that she giggled and said that she couldn't wait to read the story of my life. She didn't giggle when I told her about its theme, though, and put her arm around my shoulders and said, "Cilla, sweetheart, I know it's a lot to get used to. If there's anything you want to talk about, I'm always here."

This was convenient, because I actually did want to talk about something, which was, "Could we please get Choco-Rex cereal instead of just corn-flakes?" (Because our no-sugary cereal rule is silly, and Choco-Rex has marshmallows shaped like dinosaurs AND turns regular milk into chocolate milk *inside the bowl*.) My mom didn't say yes, but she didn't say no either. She just blinked and looked kind of confused, so I think there's hope.

But back to my family. Having my grandparents so close is GREAT, because it means I have six people to take care of me and play with me and hear my stories *all the time*. Plus I get six of every-thing, like birthday gifts and cookies and hugs when I scrape myself. Of course, I also have six people who won't hesitate to say, "Priscilla Lee-Jenkins, what are you doing, Young Lady?!" and recently, six people saying, "So, are you excited to be a big sister?" (The answer is NO.)

But it also means that, in very, very difficult situations, I have six members of my family to help me.

Like when I had to deal with the Forces of Darkness, which, when I was little, I was sure lived in my closet.

See, I don't like closets. I'm not afraid of them anymore, now that I'm eight and a half. But on nights like tonight, when I'm lying in bed writing because I can't fall asleep and the dark is sometimes scary, I have to admit that I still think they're Highly Suspicious. Why build a small room just for your clothes? Why hang your clothes up when they're so much easier to find in piles on your floor? This is just asking for trouble. If you build a small, dark room and then put a door in front of it, whatever it's hiding isn't going to be very nice.

Looking at my closet door, it's easy to remember how scared I felt when I was little. Because when my parents said good night and the light turned off, I *knew* there were monsters in my closet, waiting. I imagined big, slimy monsters, with tails and horns and smelly feet. I imagined tiny monsters, no higher than my socks. And I'd call for my mom and dad, because even small monsters are scary.

My mom would say, "Cilla, there are no such things as monsters," and my dad would open the closet and say, "See? Monster free. Feel better now?"

But the answer was *no*, because *everyone* knows that monsters learn to hide themselves when they're in monster school.

My parents would kiss me on the cheek and leave. I'd lie, waiting, and then something would rustle, or I'd imagine something had rustled, or was about to rustle.

So I'd call my parents and begin the whole thing all over again. Night after night. And nothing they could say or do would make me feel any better. Which is when my grandparents got involved.

"Monsters in the closet?" my Grandma Jenkins said, putting her hands on her hips and frowning. "Nonsense. You should just let her be," she said, turning to my mom.

But my mom didn't like that idea.

My Nai Nai said, "There are no such things as monsters. Such an imagination." She made a *tsk*-ing noise and shook her head.

And even my Grandpa Jenkins, who my grandma says will believe *anything* (which means he's the BEST kind of reader there is), told me, "You know, the monsters are just made up. Like all your other stories. Hey, maybe you could make up a story about your monsters, and imagine that they're friendly. . . ."

But this wasn't helpful either, because monsters are Serious Business—you can't just control them with a story. And monsters ARE NOT friendly. These people.

Which is when my Ye Ye invited me to come

with him to run errands, which I sometimes do because I like to hear his stories, and because he needs my help picking out new ties (never green, sometimes blue, polka dots always a plus).

But that day, Ye Ye didn't drive us to the tie shop, or the bookstore, or the tailor, or any of the places we usually go. Instead, we went to a big store with frames and mirrors everywhere, and over to a wall filled with metal poster racks.

"So, Cilla," Ye Ye said, looking serious as he flipped through the racks. "You are having trouble with monsters."

"I know, I know." I sighed. "They aren't real, I'm being silly, there's no such thing—"

"Well," Ye Ye interrupted me, but nicely. "I don't know for sure."

"Really?" I looked at him, eyes wide.

"Really." Ye Ye shrugged. "Monsters are tricky. So I have an idea. Just in case there are bad things—"

"Slimy things," I added.

"Smelly things?" he asked.

"Yes," I confirmed. "With big feet."

"Well, just in case there are any slimy, scaly, big-feet monsters, we can do something to fight them. Maybe . . ." He flipped through the rack and held up a poster. "This one?"

And there was a picture of a unicorn, big and bright and standing by a purple forest.

"It's beautiful," I gasped.

"Well," Ye Ye said, "we'll get it, and frame it, and it will hang—"

"On my closet door!" I said, finally under-standing.

"Then," Ye Ye went on, "*if* there are monsters, the unicorn will—"

"Fight them off!" I cried.

"Exactly," he said. "Using its magical horn."

"And the powers of the moon," I exclaimed.

"And the stars," he added.

"To send the Forces of Darkness back into the closet!" I finished, triumphantly.

My Ye Ye smiled, mussing my hair. "So smart."

So Ye Ye and I got a sparkly silver frame for
the poster. Then we went home and hung my
unicorn right smack dab on the closet door (high

enough to catch tall monsters, low enough to catch tiny ones—we were expert monster hunters by this point). Then we celebrated with ice cream. Every night after that, when my parents tucked me in and said good night, my unicorn took care of anything that came her way.

And that's the story of how I, Cilla Lee-Jenkins, discovered that I have the best Ye Ye ever. One who understands the power of unicorns, and also, the importance of taking action when dealing with the Forces of Darkness, even if they're *probably* not there.

And even though, every once in a loooooong while, I still ask my dad to check the closet before I go to sleep, you'll be pleased to know that I don't believe in monsters anymore.

But I definitely believe in unicorns.

# BABIES, BALDNESS, AND OTHER STRUGGLES

I saw a picture of the baby today. It's black and white, and looks like a bunch of dark circles smooshed together. I've decided to call it "The Blob."

My parents were excited to show me the picture, and to tell me that it's a girl. I don't know why they think this will make a difference. (Though it does help with name ideas. Maybe "The Sister from the Black Lagoon.") My mom kept telling me that she wishes she'd had a sister instead of just older brothers, and my dad kept saying that he has a little sister too, who is my Auntie Eva. But that's TOTALLY different, because Auntie Eva is nice and tells funny jokes and can drive and takes me bowling when she comes to visit, and the new baby isn't going to do any of those things. So I don't know why they thought that would help.

They also kept saying things like, "Do you want me to tell you about it?" and "Want to take a closer look?" even though I kept saying "no" because the picture was boring, plus I don't care.

My Grandma and Grandpa Jenkins came over in the morning to see the picture and brought coffee cake to celebrate, and then my Nai Nai and Ye Ye came over in the afternoon and brought red bean cupcakes and almond cookies, because now that she's having a baby my mom wants to eat almond cookies ALL THE TIME. This is mostly great because when she eats almond cookies, I eat them too. Though they used to be *my* favorite and are now also The Blob's favorite, apparently. Which doesn't seem fair.

After everyone left, my mom put the picture of The Blob on the refrigerator in case anyone wants to take a closer look later (which is ridiculous, because who wants to look at that?). Also, we don't *need* anything else on the refrigerator—it's already decorated with the picture I drew in class last week. I call it *Dragons Dancing in Tiaras*, and my dad said it's "certainly original" and "one of my most creative works of art yet."

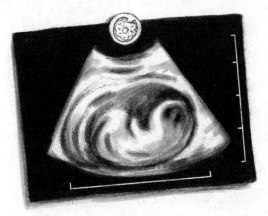

While my mom hung the photo, my dad sat on the couch with me and said, "Cilla Lee-Jenkins, your mom and I are so proud of the way you've been helping us get ready for the baby. I know you're going to be a great big sister."

And even though I knew I was supposed to say, "Thank you, Daddy, I can't wait!" what I really wanted to say was "But it's a giant blob and why is it shaped so funny and is that what it's going to look like when it comes out of Mom's stomach? Because that's gross."

So I didn't say anything. I just put my head on my dad's shoulder, and he put his arm around me and cuddled, which is always nice. He said he was excited to read my book, and he asked if I wanted to talk about anything, and I think that my case for Choco-Rex cereal is getting better, because when I finished he said, "Oh, Cilla, there's never a dull moment." Which means I did an excellent job with my argument, because boring is the WORST thing to be.

Now my mom's napping, because The Blob makes her tired ALL THE TIME. My dad's putting The Blob's crib together, and even though he said I could keep him company, he's changed his mind and wants me to play by myself for a while. (Apparently it's not helpful when I put a baby sock on my nose and run around pretending to be an elephant.)

But at least he said I could have another red bean cupcake if I promised not to make noise, and sat at the kitchen table while I ate, and tried not to get crumbs everywhere. I'm doing an EXCELLENT job, by the way. I'm putting all my crumbs in a big pile at the corner of the table, so they're not everywhere at all—just in one place.

While I'm here, I thought I'd write more of my bestselling life story. Because even though The Blob doesn't look like much, I need to finish my book and be world-famous before it's born. Just in case.

To be honest, I don't understand why my whole family made such a big deal about the picture. When I first heard about it, I thought I'd at least be able to see the baby's face, and if it looked nice. I even thought it might be waving hello, which I'd like because then I'd know it was excited to meet me and happy to be my sister. But it's just sitting there. Like blobs do.

And if it's not excited to meet me, I don't know

why I should be excited to meet *it*. Plus, even though I tell Alien-Face McGee that girls are better than boys ALL THE TIME, I was actually kind of hoping The Blob would be a boy, because my mom calls me her "special girl," and what if she decides The Blob is special too?

But at least there's ONE thing I can see from the picture of The Blob that I'm happy about (even if the rest of it is *very* disappointing).

From what I can tell, The Blob has absolutely, positively *no hair*.

Which is very good news.


You see, I don't remember much (or anything) about being a baby. But I know there were some things I was very good at. For example, I learned how to talk early on, which isn't surprising from a future bestselling author.

Soon after that, I learned about something called "quiet time" and that it's Not Acceptable to do things like wake your mom up screaming her name in the middle of the night. Which makes her run down the hallway to your room, thinking something's wrong and you're being kidnapped or dying or eaten by a shark, only to find you standing up in your crib, holding on to the bars, and saying, "Mommy, let's talk." My mom was Not Happy the one time this happened. Which I can understand now (though in my defense, I probably did have something interesting to say).

My point is that I was an excellent baby, what my Grandpa Jenkins calls "a great kid" (though sometimes I'm also what he calls "a pill," but we won't go into that).

But there's one thing that wasn't so great about me as a baby, something you can see in all the photos. For all the greatness and talent inside my head, the outside of my head was a mess. As if being named Priscilla Lee-Jenkins wasn't bad enough, when I was little, I was bald. And being bald is a hard way to enter the world.

Being bald means people in the park stop your mom and say things like, "What's his name? He's just precious!"

"You mean the little boy in the green dress?" my mom would answer.

The doctors said I'd grow out of it, but the problem didn't go away. By the time I was almost four, even my grandparents, who think I'm the most beautiful grandchild on Earth, were beginning to notice.

"Does this happen a lot in America?" my Nai Nai asked, looking suspiciously at my mom's hair. "Ay yah!" (This is the Chinese way of saying "My goodness!" or "Oh no!")

"She looks like an old man," my Ye Ye said, rubbing my head.

My Grandma Jenkins started patting my mom's shoulder whenever we came over, and saying things like "Not to worry, dear, she has personality." (But I don't know what that has to do with my hair.)

Of course, I wanted hair. But I was so little that at first, I didn't really notice that I was bald and everyone else wasn't. For a long time, I didn't mind it THAT much.

But then, the summer when I was four, which means my head was still mostly bald with a small patch of fuzz around the edges, my cousin Helen came to visit.

My cousin Helen is my age, which means that my Grandma Jenkins thinks we should play together and be "as thick as thieves." But I don't like playing with Helen because she bosses me around, plus I'm not a thief (I'm a future author extraordinaire).

Helen lives far away, and every summer, her mom and dad send her to spend a whole MONTH with my Grandma and Grandpa Jenkins. While she's here, she goes to a special summer camp for kids who play music (I wanted to go to this camp too, because I'm EXCELLENT at the kazoo, but apparently that doesn't count). When Helen's here,

I have to share the playroom, which is usually just for *me*, and my grandparents always throw her a birthday party with all her friends from the special camp, who make me feel shy.

And as if all of this wasn't bad enough, that summer, Helen had hair so long, it reached *below her shoulders.*

She wore long, light brown braided *pigtails* that she held together with matching *bows.*

When she took the bows and the pigtails out, her hair fell into perfect corkscrew *curls.*

This was just too much. Bows *and* pigtails *and* curls? When you're bald and your mom is trying to tape a bow to your head because it won't stay on, then and only then will you understand the agony of this terrible injustice.

Of course, I didn't blame Helen for having brown curly pigtails. That's not something you can control.

But I did, absolutely, positively, no question about it, blame her for the princess party.

* * *

**A princess-themed birthday party** should be a great thing, and I was excited when I heard that Helen wanted one. Playing princesses is one of the best games out there, especially when Colleen and I play it at recess. We take turns being princesses and dragons, and sometimes we even pretend that we're princess dragons, which is an excellent game because you get to wear a crown AND breathe fire.

I'd invented an AMAZING princess story too. My name, I decided, was Catherina Rosalindia Lightningglass, and I was the princess of a kingdom where everyone rode sparkly blue horses and sometimes grew wings. It was a very good story. I was dressed in my very special princess dress, which was sparkly purple and even had a lacy skirt underneath.

When I got to the party, Helen was standing with a group of girls from camp, laughing by the goody bag table. She was wearing a pink and yellow princess dress, and her hair was braided in pigtails tied with matching yellow bows.

And on the top of her head, she wore a beautiful, sparkly, silver tiara that *clipped onto her hair.*

"Hi, Cilla." Helen waved when she saw me. She reached over to the goody bags and took something silver out. "We got crowns for everyone. Sorry you can't wear yours," she said, making a face and handing the crown to me. Behind her, I could hear her friends giggling. "But your dress is pretty," Helen said, trying to sound encouraging. "We almost match!" Just then someone called her name, and as Helen and all her friends walked off, I heard one of the girls say, "What kind of princess doesn't have hair?"

I watched Helen walk away, her princess dress swishing. I touched my bald head. Even though I was wearing my very special princess dress, I suddenly didn't feel like a princess, and I was sure I didn't look like one. Catherina Rosalindia Lightningglass didn't seem like such a great name anymore either. It even felt a little silly. My bald head would stand out next to all the sparkling tiaras.

Unless . . .

Then I was running, away from the party, up the stairs to the playroom. I opened the arts and crafts drawer and pulled out a great big bottle of glue. Smearing glue all over the bottom of the tiara (also my fingers and possibly the floor), I closed my eyes, held the crown high above me, and with a deep breath *squished* it down hard, pressing it to my head.

"Priscilla Lee-Jenkins, *what are you doing*?"

I spun around. My Grandma Jenkins stood in the doorway. And she was Not Happy.

I gave her my best "who me?" look, but that wasn't a good strategy, because the tiara slid to the floor, which left a gluey mess across my head and down my dress.

Now, I know I'm a literary genius with a great and epic future ahead of me, but this was all a little too much. So I burst into tears. I told my grandma the whole story, starting with Catherina Rosalindia Lightningglass and the wings and Helen's friends and the baldness. I think she stopped me somewhere around "taking my destiny into my own hands." (I probably didn't quite say this, since I was four, but I *meant* it, so that's what I'm writing here. This is called Creative License, which means that if you're an artist, you can change things that happen in real life to make them more interesting. I use it a lot.)

"Come now, dear." She gave me a hug, or a sort of hug, because the glue was all over me and had smeared more while I cried. "Of course you can be a princess."

"No," I wailed. "Princesses aren't bald, and if the tiara won't stay on, I definitely won't be a princess. Also, I have glue on my head so now I'm going to be funny-looking *and* sticky."

My Grandma Jenkins took a long, deep breath.

Then *my* grandma—my "no messes," "no silliness," "no nonsense, Young Lady" Grandma Jenkins—went over to the arts and crafts drawer, looked through it for a minute, and pulled out a small jar.

"Well," she said, with a sigh, but also a funny kind of smile at the corner of her mouth, "we can do something about that."

And so I, Cilla Lee-Jenkins, future author extraordinaire, descended the staircase, my grandma behind me, with a head that sparkled—no, *dazzled*—with glue and the half a jar of glitter Grandma Jenkins had poured over me, plus a few star stickers we'd found at the bottom of the drawer.

"Good afternoon, Princess Helen," I said, when I reached the bottom of the staircase.

"Cilla!" Helen didn't know what to say. "You look, you look . . ."

"Like a princess?" my grandma suggested.

"Like Cinderella at the ball!" Helen exclaimed. "Right after her fairy godmother used her magic!"

And I'll admit it—I realized right then that I liked Helen maybe just a little.

Though I still think the bows were a bit much.

* * *

**It was a long time before my hair grew to a** normal length (though now it's *past my shoulders,* which is probably the most exciting thing that's ever happened to me, other than being destined for literary greatness). But after that day, I didn't worry about it anymore (or at least, as much). My mom let me decorate my head with stickers in place of bows. And sometimes, for very special occasions, she let me draw on my head with markers.

But even though being bald wasn't all that bad in the end, when I look at The Blob's photo, I can't help but stare very hard at it. In fact, I got up, just a minute ago, to take a closer look. I had to stand on a chair to reach it, and I put my finger against it, and followed all the lines of the picture. I don't *think* I saw any hair. Though there was one line that looked like it maybe could be, might possibly be, the start of a pigtail. Which would be AWFUL.

So I took destiny into my own hands.

# MY BRUSH WITH DESTINY, OR HOW I BECAME A FUTURE AUTHOR EXTRAORDINAIRE

**Today on the playground, my best friend Colleen** and I talked about what we're going to be when we grow up, which is also known as destiny. Destinies are GREAT things to have, because they mean that you already know what you're going to do with your life, so you don't have to worry about it anymore. This is nice, because there are so many other things to worry about (like making friends and being afraid of the dark). Colleen wanted to know all about how I knew I'd be an author, which was fun to tell. She's not sure about her destiny yet, but it'll probably involve robots and space travel. We're both very excited for this, because when she's a world-famous astronaut, I'll write stories about her adventures and it will be AMAZING.

Playing destinies with Colleen made me realize that there's an important story I haven't told you yet. Because the whole point of this book is that I'm a future author extraordinaire. So I should tell you the story of how I found this out, before you wonder if we'll ever get to it.

It all started one day at the grocery store. My mom was paying the cashier and I was waiting for her by the gumball machine. I was maybe five years old, which means my hair was just past my ears, and I was imagining what would happen if I melted all the gumballs into one giant gumball, and what color it would be, and how long it would take to chew, when I was interrupted by a person who can only be described as a Rude Individual.

This is true for several reasons. First, she interrupted me when I was clearly concentrating, which is rude. But what's even worse is that she interrupted me to say, "Oh my goodness, look at you!"

She bent down next to me, which was NOT appropriate. We're strangers, so if I'm not supposed to talk to them, it doesn't seem fair that they're allowed to talk to me.

"Aren't you something special!" she exclaimed. "What an interesting face you've got there! Those *eyes*!"

Now *that* is rude. If there's one thing I know in this world, it's that you don't comment on people's faces. Like this woman, who had lips that puckered like a fish and wore bright orange glasses that matched her bright orange hair (and not in a good way). It wouldn't have been appropriate to say something about her face, even when it looked like *that*, because people take their faces personally and you don't want to hurt their feelings. That's why, when I call Ben McGee "Alien-Face McGee," I don't do it because his face looks anything like an alien's. I call him that because I've made up a story about how he's an alien who was sent here to spy on us in human disguise, which means his Alien-Face lurks underneath waiting to burst forth. Though that's a longer story for later.

*Anyway,* I'm a Polite Individual, so I didn't tell this woman that talking to strangers, staring at my face, and then calling it names meant that she was being a rude one. I just didn't look at her, and looked instead at my mom, who was trying to get the clerk to hurry.

"Who's that?" the woman asked, clearly not good at reading looks. "Is that your mommy? Well, she must be so pleased to have such an unusual daughter. Now, what are you, exactly?"

The question startled me.

It was a big question, and it made me think. *What was I?*

No one had ever asked me this before. I wasn't a "Priscilla," that's for sure, and I was much more than a "Lee-Jenkins." I was a daughter, and a girl, but lots of people are daughters and girls, so that wasn't enough. I wanted to be something special. I wanted to be something *great*.

And this was my moment.

My chance.

To declare myself to the world, to decide who I was.

What was I, Cilla Lee-Jenkins? What did I want to be?

And then it happened. An answer came, bubbling up from deep inside me.

"I," I said, breathless with the wondrousness of it all, "am a future author extraordinaire."

I expected a big reaction, as I'd just realized my destiny of greatness, right then and there by the gumball machine. But the Rude Individual, it turns out, was also not very bright, and just looked confused.

"No, dear, I mean *what* are you?"

But then my mom was suddenly there next to me. "Can I help you?" she said, taking my hand.

"I was just asking your fascinating daughter what she was. You don't see looks like that normally, and I just *had* to know."

"Well, you heard her, didn't you?" My mom was polite, but her words were careful and clipped, so the Rude Individual would understand. "She is a future author extraordinaire."

Then my mom said, "Come on, Cilla," in a sing-songy voice, and we got to the car and she put me in my car seat, and said, in a short, funny way, "Well, what a *Rude Individual*." And then we went to the ice cream store and got cones with sprinkles.

And the very next day, I got a present—a sign of my very own to hang outside my bedroom door, which was painted blue and said in big, white letters: "Priscilla Lee-Jenkins, Future Author Extraordinaire."

Which, as I told Colleen today at recess, goes to show you that even though parents can make AWFUL decisions (like having Blobs, and calling me Priscilla, and saying that there's not-a-chance-on-earth-young-lady that they'll agree to name the baby Glimmerella), they're not *all* bad. And *sometimes*, parents get it right.

# PRESCHOOL BLUES

**Today, my Nai Nai took me to the craft store.**
She's making pillows and curtains for The Blob's
room, and wanted my help choosing the fabric.

The Blob is going to have the small room across
from mine, which we used before to hold books. So
far, there's a crib and a rocking chair inside, but
otherwise it's pretty empty. The rocking chair is
fun, but I wish the books were still there instead of
in boxes in the hall (I liked to play in that room,
and pretend it was a cave).

Shopping was okay, mostly because Nai Nai said
she'd make me new pillows too, because being a Big
Sister is something to celebrate. This isn't true,

of course, but I love it when my Nai Nai makes me things. She makes all of our curtains, which is very special, especially because Grandma Jenkins says that good custom-made curtains are impossible to find these days. I keep telling her that Nai Nai would be happy to make her some too, but she never remembers to call. But maybe she will when I show her the new pillows Nai Nai's going to make for me, which will be AMAZING because I picked out fabric that's blue with sparkly penguins on it. I wasn't sure what to pick for The Blob, mostly because I still don't want it moving into my house. But my Nai Nai found white fabric with ladybugs on it, which I like.

After the store, we went to Chinatown for lunch, which is always great. Nai Nai orders my favorite foods, and we eat with chopsticks. I love chopsticks, though they took me awhile to learn how to use. But now I'm EXCELLENT at them, and Nai Nai is very proud.

While we waited for our food, we took the chopsticks out of their paper wrappers and folded the paper back and forth, like a fan, to make chopstick holders. After we ate, we got bowls of sweet soup made of beans for dessert, which I was allowed to slurp. In fact, no one minds if you slurp your soup in Chinatown (which I can't do at home), and no one cares if your elbows are on the table (my Grandma Jenkins is VERY concerned about this). There are some special rules that you *do* have to learn, though. For example, when the check comes all the grown-ups have to fight over who's going to pay it (which is funny to watch), and you can NEVER put extra soy sauce on your food.

I love mostly everything about Chinatown. I love the sound of Chinese, even though I don't understand it. I love the fish with big heads and wide eyes that swim in a tank by the door. And I love the food, which comes on big, steaming plates that we put in the middle of the table and share.

Today, though, just as my Nai Nai and I sat down, a waiter walked by with a plate of something familiar for another table, something that I used to love, but don't anymore. I haven't thought about it in a long time. My Nai Nai saw it too, and looked at me with her eyebrow raised and a question on her face. But I just said, "No thank you."

Now I'm home, and my mom is working at her desk. I'm lying on the fuzzy rug next to her, because I can keep her company on the condition that I work too, and don't talk or bother her. I've been pretty good at this so far, and only interrupted once to ask if she ever lies on the rug, because it's so comfortable. And when she said no, to ask her why not. And maybe a third time to tell her about how someday I'll have a desk of my own, because all serious writers do. But I'll also have a fuzzy rug like this one, because I love it so much. But that's it.

At first, I wasn't sure what I'd write about this afternoon (other than the rug). But I can't stop thinking about Chinatown, or that plate. They have a story all their own. And this story happened when my hair was just long enough for bows but still too short for pigtails, when I went to a place called preschool.

\* \* \*

**Preschool is a fun place.** Your mom drops you off in the morning and you're a big girl about it, but really you don't want her to go because even though you're brave you have a stomachache and pneumonia and leprosy and will miss her. But once you've hung up your backpack and put your lunchbox in your cubby, you feel better.

Plus Miss Jill is there to give you a hug and say, "Why don't we go play with the puppets?"

And afterward, you forget about your stomachache and pneumonia, because preschool is mostly great.

However, there is one drawback to preschool—*other kids.*

I found this out one day when we were sitting around the sharing rug, which was a rug decorated with the letters of the alphabet where we took turns going around in a circle and saying our favorite things. On this particular day, Miss Jill asked us to share our favorite foods.

It was an easy question, and I was excited to answer, because if you can't get excited about food, then what else is there? I had a big smile on my face when I shared my answer too, because sharing was my favorite part of the day, and I loved thinking about my favorite food, which my Nai Nai always ordered especially for me when we were in Chinatown.

So I said, "Snails."

"What?" shrieked a girl with long pigtails.

"Snails," I said, confused that she hadn't understood the first time.

"But . . . what do you eat?" another boy said, and didn't even look embarrassed that he hadn't been listening.

"Snails."

"Like . . . with shells?" a boy with a pipsqueak voice asked.

In the literary world, this is what's known as a Tough Crowd.

I looked at Miss Jill, because they all clearly had some sort of brain fever that made you forget animal names, and probably needed to go to the hospital. But Miss Jill looked confused, not worried, like she was putting on a brave face before leaving to call the ambulance.

So I put on a brave face too. "Yes," I said, gently.

*"Eeeeeeeeeeewwwwwwww,"* they all said.

This wasn't the reaction I was expecting.

"Now, guys," Miss Jill cut in. "That isn't very nice. I'm sure Cilla can explain."

I looked at her, surprised. Had she caught the brain sickness too? "Explain what?" I asked, but my voice had suddenly gotten a bit smaller and higher, and I had a feeling in my stomach like I'd done something wrong.

"What you mean by snails. You don't eat real snails, right? Maybe candy ones?"

"No," I whispered, wishing it wasn't my turn anymore. "Just . . . real snails."

"Oh," Miss Jill said. "How interesting. Um, where do you even get those?"

"Chinatown," I said, my voice all funny.

"Oh," Miss Jill said again. "Well, thank you for sharing, Cilla. Ryan, why don't you share next?" And then the conversation was over, but the other kids were giggling, and my face was burning and I suddenly didn't like sharing time as much as I used to.

When my dad picked me up from school that afternoon, I didn't know I was still thinking about it. But when he said, "You're awfully quiet today, Cilla. Everything okay?" I found myself asking, "Dad, are we Chinese?"

"Uh, yes, sweetie. We are." My dad pushed his glasses higher on his nose, which is what he does whenever he's thinking or nervous. "I'm Chinese, and your Nai Nai and Ye Ye are Chinese, and you're half Chinese."

"Oh," I said. I'd known this, I guess, but I'd never really thought about it before. And then something else occurred to me.

"But does being half Chinese mean that I'm not really Chinese?"

"No," my dad said, firmly. "It means that you *are* Chinese, but also something else. You're as Chinese as me and your Nai Nai and Ye Ye, but you're also Caucasian, like your mom. Which means you get to be both things, which is very special."

I had to think about this for a while.

"Okay," I said, finally. "But, Dad?"

"Yes, sweetheart?"

"I don't think I like snails anymore."

The next time we went to Chinatown, my Nai Nai ordered snails even though I didn't want them. And when I had a bite, because my mom and dad insisted, I decided I didn't like them.

"Ewww, *gross*," I said.

My mom said, "But, Cilla, you love snails."

My dad said, "How about you try another bite?"

But I said no, because suddenly the taste had become something bad, though I didn't want to say that because I didn't want to hurt my Nai Nai's feelings.

My Nai Nai looked at me for a moment, not

like she was angry, but like she was trying to figure something out. "This happens with children," she said, finally. "Tastes change. Here." She called over the waiter. A few minutes later, a plate of something hot and delicious-smelling and new came to our table. "Bamboo hearts," she said. "Try."

They were flat, soft vegetables that came on top of a pile of steaming hot spinach. I poked at them with my chopsticks. They smelled good. And they didn't seem like something that anyone at preschool would call "gross," no matter how little imagination they might have. I took a bite.

"Yum!" I said.

"Yay," my dad said.

"I want to try some," my mom said.

"A favorite?" my Nai Nai asked.

"Yes." I smiled back.

"It's my favorite, too," she said. "Much better than snails. It's a very special, grown-up food."

"Wow!" I exclaimed. This was a big deal. "Also," I said, "did you know that we're both Chinese?"

"Yes," my Nai Nai replied, patting my hand with her soft, papery one. "Have some more."

**Bamboo hearts are called tzuck sang in Chinese,** and I get them every time I go to Chinatown, including today. They're delicious, and my Nai Nai always gives me the last piece, even when I say I'm too full. Which is VERY nice of her, since they're her favorite too.

But I never had snails again, which is maybe a little sad.

Or at least, that's how I felt, suddenly, at lunch today, when I saw that plate of snails go by.

I think my Nai Nai understood, though. When I said no and got quiet, she took my hand and asked me to tell her more about my book. Nai Nai didn't know what a bestseller was, so I had to explain that it's a book you write if you want to be famous. Everyone will buy it (because it sells the "best," obviously).

"Ay yah!" she said, when I told her.

"I know," I said with a big smile. "It will be GREAT."

And then, even though we were just talking about books, she said that no matter how busy things got with the baby, she and my Ye Ye would always have time to play with me, and to listen to my stories.

After lunch, she surprised me with an order of tzuck sang just for me, which came wrapped in a small container, to take to school for lunch the next day. This was very exciting because I've never had tzuck sang all to myself. Plus, when I brought leftovers from Chinatown to school for lunch last year, which I was kind of nervous to do, Colleen tried them and LOVED them. And if she AND my Nai Nai love something, it means it definitely and officially can't be gross. So tomorrow, Colleen and I will be able to share tzuck sang, and I bet she'll even let me have one of the chocolate cookies her mom packs in the special dessert pocket of her lunchbox.

Which means that this chapter can come to a happy, delicious end.

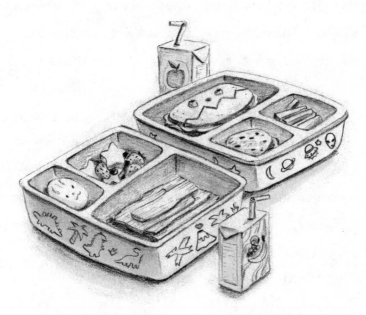

# KINDERGARTEN AND OTHER TRAGEDIES

**When you're upset, you're supposed to use** your words to say why. My mom and dad tell me this all the time (though every once in a while when they yell, my mom says, "For heaven's sake, Nathan, use your words." So I think it's something they have to work on too.).

But sometimes, when you're sitting at recess by yourself, and life is awful, and your best friend hates you, and you're thinking that maybe you should move somewhere far away like Alaska or Zanzibar, *and* you spilled milk at lunch and now your socks are making a squishy sound, it can be VERY hard to find the words you need.

Now, you'd think that being a literary genius would make me excellent at expressing myself. Of course, sometimes it does. For example, I've used my words to call the baby in my mom's stomach Blobzilla, even though my parents have already picked out its name. They keep saying that it's Not Acceptable to call my little sister The Blob or any of the other excellent names I've come up with. (Whatever happens, though, I won't call the new baby by the name my parents have picked. I hate it. In fact, I hate it so much, I won't write it down here. So there.)

But sometimes, being a future author extraordinaire doesn't help with words at all, *especially* when you're upset. Like yesterday, when I found out some TERRIBLE NEWS about The Blob, even worse than knowing that it's coming at all.

I've mostly been trying to forget about The Blob over these past few weeks. Its room is slowly getting decorated (and I'll admit that the pillows my Nai Nai made look very nice, though my penguin pillows are MUCH better). But otherwise, not much has happened with it, and I haven't wanted to talk about it. And it's been fun pretending like nothing's going to change.

So when my mom came back from a doctor's appointment and asked me to sit down on the couch with her, I hoped it would be about something completely unrelated to The Blob. Maybe she wanted to talk about painting the house purple (I'm always pushing for this), or buying a pony (this too), or quitting her job to open up an ice cream store (which would be GREAT, and I'd visit every day).

But then she said, "Cilla, I need to tell you something," in a serious voice, and I knew I wouldn't like this conversation. "The doctors did some tests to make sure the baby's healthy, which it is," my mom went on. "But they realized they got the due date wrong, which means the baby's going to be coming a bit later than we'd thought. This means that if the baby takes a while, there's a chance that it's going to be born just before school starts, around your birthday."

It took me a minute to understand what she meant.

"I wanted to let you know, sweetheart," my mom went on. "There's a very good chance that the baby will be born before then. And even if it's born close to your birthday, it will still be your special day."

"But," I tried to find my words (it was very hard). "But it won't be born *on* my birthday, right?"

"It's really unlikely," my mom said, "really." But that wasn't a good answer, because the only good answer to that question is "NO."

My mom asked if I wanted to talk, and for once the answer to that was also "no." Because how do you find the words to say how unfair it is that The Blob with the terrible name is not only taking your favorite food, and your parents, and your grandparents, and the room where you used to play cave, but now it wants your birthday too?

My mom was still trying to talk about my feelings this morning while we walked to the bus, but I didn't want to. In fact, all I wanted to do was talk to Colleen about what my mom had told me, because Colleen always knows what to say, and is on my side, and I hoped she'd tell me that The Blob is AWFUL, which would be nice to hear.

But then things got even worse.

When Colleen got on the bus, something was different. She wasn't smiling like usual, and she didn't say "Hi" or "Cilla!" or "I have the *best* story to tell you" or any of the things she normally does when I see her in the morning.

Instead, she sat down next to me with a small sigh.

"Hi, Colleen," I said quickly. "I have the WORST news." And I told her about The Blob.

And I waited for her to tell me it was going to be okay.

But she didn't.

Instead, she just crossed her arms and made a sighing sound.

"Isn't that the worst thing *ever*?" I prodded.

"*No,*" Colleen said, suddenly, in an exasperated voice. "It's not."

I was surprised, and the bottom of my eyes got hot and itchy, and I didn't know what to say, or what I'd done wrong.

"Sorry," Colleen said, after a minute. "It's just that my grandpa called last night. My grandma fell and hurt her hip."

"Oh," I said.

"She's okay," Colleen went on, "but she has to go to the hospital and have an operation."

"Oh," I said again. And I wanted to say something more. But I didn't know what, and I wanted to make everything better for Colleen, but I didn't know how, and what did it even mean to fall and break a hip, and the word "hospital" made my stomach do a flip, and—

Colleen was looking at me, like she expected something. So I said, "Oh," again, quietly. And then there was another, longer pause, and I tried to find something to say to make everything okay.

But before I could, Colleen looked away, and said, "She'll be fine," in a short, funny voice. "But excuse me if I don't want to talk about The Blob *again*," she went on, with her arms crossed. "You'll just have to deal with it on your own and not be such a baby."

And I still didn't know what to say. So I didn't say anything.

We were quiet on the bus after that. We didn't play or talk like we usually do. And I couldn't look at Colleen, and I wanted to give her a hug. But I also wanted to tell her that she hadn't been fair.

I spent the rest of the bus ride, and all of circle time and math, trying to think of the things I should have said. Some of them were angry, but most of them were sorry. And then, before we had a chance to talk, while I was paired with Alien-Face McGee for reading, I looked across the room to where Colleen had been sitting with Tim #1, and she was *gone*.

I thought maybe she'd been abducted by aliens

or trolls (which was more likely, since Alien-Face was with me the whole time). Actually, I sort of wish it *had* been trolls, because then I could have rescued her, and she'd be sorry that she'd ever said anything mean, and she'd know I cared about her and her grandma. But that's not what happened.

Instead, when I asked Ms. Bloom where Colleen was, she said that Colleen had a stomachache, and was waiting with the nurse for her mom to pick her up. Ms. Bloom looked surprised too, and said, "Oh, I thought she'd told you, Cilla," because Colleen and I tell each other EVERYTHING. But Colleen left without telling me. Colleen left *without saying goodbye*.

Which I guess means that Colleen doesn't want to be my friend anymore.

**So I'm sitting by the swings, by myself, writing.** Alien-Face invited me to play on the balance beam with him and Tim #1, but I said NO, because how could I play at a time like this? Also, Colleen loves balance beams, so it would make me think of her and be sad.

I haven't been this upset, or alone on the playground, or TERRIBLE with my words, for a long time. And sitting here feels a lot like it did the first time I found out that you can be really, really bad with your words, literary genius or not.

It all started in kindergarten.


**Kindergarten is a big deal. It's your first time** at real school, and your first time riding the bus. Plus, when I went to kindergarten, my hair was so long that for the first time in my life it TOUCHED MY SHOULDERS.

So I was happy about going to kindergarten, right up till the morning I had to get ready for the school bus for the first time.

Then several things occurred to me.

First, there would be older kids there. I have a strict policy against older kids. This is because:

1. I worry they'll be mean.
2. I worry they'll squish me on purpose.
3. I worry they'll squish me by accident, even if they're not mean, because these things can happen.

I was also reconsidering this bus business. Yes, it was yellow and exciting, but there would be older kids on it too (see above), I wouldn't know anyone, and what if I didn't know where to get off and accidentally stayed on for too long and ended up in another school, or state, or country, and never found my way home?

When my mom came upstairs and found me in my pajamas saying "No thank you, Mommy. I've decided I don't want to go to kindergarten," she wasn't as sympathetic as she could've been. In fact, she wasn't sympathetic at all.

But when I finally came downstairs, dressed and ready to go, I told her my real fear, the actual thing that was the scariest about kindergarten, even worse than big kids. "But," I asked my mom, "what if no one likes me and I don't make any *friends*?"

And my mom knelt down so our faces were very close, and she held out her arms so I could cuddle into her shoulder, which is my favorite thing, and she said, "Priscilla Lee-Jenkins, you are someone worth knowing. So if anyone doesn't want to be your friend, they're missing out." She gave me a piggyback ride to the bus stop, though I got down before the bus came so everyone would know I was a big girl. I waved goodbye to my parents as the bus pulled away, and I think Mom was catching a cold because she kept blowing her nose and wiping her eyes on my dad's shirt.

The bus wasn't so bad. The big kids didn't bother

me, and I met Lou, who's still my bus driver, and very nice, and promised that he'd tell me when to get off the bus. School, however, was a different story.

My kindergarten teacher was Ms. Cotton. She had bright white hair that curved in a ball around her face just like a cotton ball, so her head matched her name, which was impressive.

Ms. Cotton smiled a lot, but didn't seem all that happy about anything. I decided that I didn't think I liked Ms. Cotton that first morning, when we played a "getting to know you game" and took turns saying our names.

"Priscilla Lee-Jenkins," I said, nearly in a whisper.

"Huh," Ms. Cotton said, finding me on her attendance sheet. "What an unusual name."

And then, before I could tell her that I wanted to be called "Cilla," not "Priscilla," she said, in a loud voice, "Class, in case you couldn't hear, this is Priscilla. She's just a bit shy." And she moved on to the next student, and no one else seemed to have the problem called "shy," and some of the kids even said funny things and made the class laugh. And I didn't like that everyone thought I was quiet and boring and a Priscilla. I wanted to turn to Ms. Cotton and say, in a loud voice, "No, I'm not shy. I'm a future author extraordinaire."

But I didn't.


**I did a lot of sitting by myself, by the swings,** during those first few days of kindergarten. I tried to play with the other kids. But even though I built a block castle with a girl named Sophie and had a monkey bar contest with Tim #1, I was always thinking and worrying about what to say. So when I played block castles, I wanted to make up stories about the people who lived inside them, but decided against it, and Sophie looked kind of bored and went to play with the bouncing balls instead. And when I played with Tim #1 on the monkey bars, he pretended to be a monkey, so I began to be an elephant who used her trunk to do monkey bar tricks. But then Tim #1 got confused because he said monkeys and elephants don't do the same things. I wanted to explain that no, I'd made up a story about an elephant and a monkey who trained together at the circus and were famous for their daring deeds. Only I suddenly didn't know if I should share my story with him, so I just said quietly, "Oh, okay. I'll be a monkey too."

I didn't have a very good time for the rest of that recess, and I think Tim #1 thought I was weird, and I *definitely* didn't seem like someone worth knowing.

So even though my dad said, "Cilla, sweetie, at least give it a week," I despaired.

As writers do.

**The only person in kindergarten who didn't** make me feel quaky and nervous inside was Ms. Lynn, the kindergarten helper, who was in our classroom every other day. Ms. Bloom reminds me of her. She had short hair that was brown and spiky and two earrings in one of her ears. She loved reading, and she told me that she used to make up stories about a platypus named Petulia who had adventures while she was at school. So I knew that Ms. Lynn had a great imagination, and an appreciation for excellent names. Also, she was very nice.

It was Ms. Lynn who would come check on me during snack time when I was sitting by myself. It was Ms. Lynn who would tell me that she liked how I used pink for the sky instead of blue, because "why not?" And it was Ms. Lynn who told us about the book project.

The book project should've been very exciting for me, since writing is my life's work and all. It went like this:

We were writing a class book.

Every student would write and illustrate one page, and your page would pick up where the last person's page left off. This meant that everyone would know a tiny bit of the story, but not the whole thing. We would take turns meeting with Ms. Lynn so she could help us with our page and show us the page that came before. Then she'd put our book together over the weekend, and Ms. Cotton would read it to the class on Monday, and it would be an exciting surprise for all of us.

I wasn't sure about the whole group-authorship thing, *especially* if Ms. Cotton was involved. And I was right to worry. Because when my turn for the book project came, not only did my page come after Billy Lane's (who, between you and me, is a Very Boring Individual), but to top it all off, Ms. Lynn was out sick that day, so Ms. Cotton herself was going to help me write it.

By this point, I knew that I didn't like Ms. Cotton, no matter how literal her hair was. And on that fateful afternoon, when she called me up to her desk, my words *vanished.*

Here is an account of what happened, told exactly how I remember it happening. This may not, however, be what Ms. Cotton would remember happening, because there's a large part of the conversation that she didn't hear:

**Ms. Cotton:** Well, Priscilla, here's what the page before yours, which Billy has written, is going to say: "And then the cat had some milk, because she was thirsty."

**Me on the Inside:** Is that it?
**Me on the Outside:** [Silence]

**Ms. Cotton:** Isn't that a nice place to build our page from?

**Me on the Inside:** No, it's actually very boring. Just like Billy.
**Me on the Outside:** [Silence]

**Ms. Cotton:** There are so many things you can imagine happening after just this one page! [She looks at me, like she's expecting something.]

**Me on the Inside:** You don't get out much, do you?
**Me on the Outside:** [Silence]

**Ms. Cotton:** So, can you think of what you'd like your page to say?

**Me on the Inside:** No.
**Me on the Outside:** [Silence]

**Ms. Cotton:** Don't worry, Priscilla, making stories is much harder than it looks.

**Me on the Inside:** Yes, I know. I Struggle with my art every day.
**Me on the Outside:** [Silence]

**Ms. Cotton:** What do you usually do after you've had a drink?

**Me on the Inside:** "Pee" is probably not the right answer. . . .
**Me on the Outside:** [Silence]

**Ms. Cotton:** Well?

**Me on the Inside:** Wait, maybe "pee" is the right answer . . . ?
**Me on the Outside:** [Silence]

**Ms. Cotton:** Do you have a snack?

**Me on the Inside:** Oh. I guess. Though I wouldn't write a story about it.
**Me on the Outside:** [Silence]

**Ms. Cotton:** Well, what if she was hungry, maybe she wanted some food to go with the milk?

**Me on the Inside:** This book isn't going to be a bestseller, is it?
**Me on the Outside:** [Silence]

**Ms. Cotton:** Well, Priscilla?

**Me on the Inside:** Art is dead.
**Me on the Outside:** [in a very small, quiet voice] Okay. She got a cookie, and then because she was very full and tired, she took a nap.

**Ms. Cotton:** Excellent! [She writes it down on a big piece of paper.] Well done. Now, you can illustrate your page during free time.

**Me on the Inside:** Sigh.
**Me on the Outside:** [very quietly] Okay.

[Exit Cilla Lee-Jenkins, stage left, in despair.]
End scene.

Despair is an excellent theme to end this chapter on. It's how I feel right now. I'm at home, writing on my mom's office rug. And when I got off the bus this afternoon, I was in so much despair that I maybe started crying (even though I didn't want to, because that's being a baby, just like Colleen said I was). And I told my dad about how Colleen's not my friend anymore, and I need to switch schools and go somewhere really far away like Alaska, and I said the wrong thing, and my feelings are hurt, and trolls would be better.

"Cilla, sweetie," my dad said, after giving me hugs, and having me take some deep breaths, and then asking me to tell the story in order with just the facts. (Apparently, it's confusing when you include the part about trolls.)

"It sounds like Colleen is having a hard time

right now," my dad went on. "She shouldn't have said what she did, and I'm sure she knows you care about her. Tomorrow, you two can apologize and talk about what happened."

But that sounds like a conversation I don't know how to have. Because it sounds like I'd need words that aren't just in my head, or aren't just a part of a story.

And I don't know if I have those.

# KINDERGARTEN, PART II.
# LESS OF A STRUGGLE,
# PLUS ROCKET SHIPS

**The school bus can be a lonely place. Colleen** isn't here. My dad talked to Colleen's mom on the phone yesterday, and they spoke about Colleen's grandma (who's okay, which was a BIG relief). And then they talked about something my dad called "trouble in paradise" (which doesn't sound good, but with all the other TERRIBLE things going on, I decided not to ask). Apparently, Colleen's feeling better and will be in school later today. But she's staying at home this morning so she can talk with her grandma on the phone before the operation.

My mom and dad said I could use my time on the bus to practice what I'd say to her. But this idea scares me. So I'm writing in my book instead.

Plus, I don't think my dad's advice right now is as good as some of the advice I've gotten from my family in the past. Like how my Nai Nai gave me advice in kindergarten, the afternoon after my conversation with Ms. Cotton.

"How is school?" she asked, as we walked to the bus stop on our way to Chinatown.

"Fine," I mumbled.

She looked down at me and raised an eyebrow.

And then the whole story spilled out, starting with, "At first I was scared of being squished," and ending with, "I'm terrible at expressing myself and doomed to a friendless existence!"

I paused to catch my breath, caught up in my story. So I was surprised when I turned to my Nai Nai and she was *smiling*.

"Ay yah," she said, as if I hadn't just told a Terrible and Awful Tale of Tragedy. "We talk, yes?"

"Of course," I said, confused, because that's the most obvious thing in the world.

"And you understand me?" she prodded.

"Yes. You're my Nai Nai."

"And you would say that you know me, yes, and I know you?"

"Well, of course." I put my hands on my hips. "But I don't understand how this—"

"Priscilla Lee-Jenkins, I do not know much English."

This startled me. "Well . . . yes," I said, finally. "But—"

"Last week, you want me to read your story, but I did not know your words. Did that stop us?"

"No," I said, thinking back. "I acted out the car chase until you understood, and we used your Chinese to English picture dictionary for the rest, and you taught me how to say 'dragon' in Chinese."

"Yes." She nodded. "See? You are so good at expressing, without words. So show what you want your class to know about you. Think about it and wah!"—this is the Chinese way of saying "presto!" or "abracadabra!" or "oh my!" "Just give it time," she concluded.

I thought about my Nai Nai's advice all through our visit to Chinatown, and during dinner, and even during the story my mom read me that night. But it wasn't until I was almost asleep that it hit me.

Wah!

Suddenly, I knew what to do.

**But that was kindergarten, not second grade.** And I didn't know what to do today, or what to say to Colleen. So when she finally got to school, just before Quiet Time, I was nervous, and even a little scared. This was extra sad, because we both LOVE Quiet Time—it's our favorite part of the day. During Quiet Time we sit and read, and usually I'm very excited about it, and nothing (or almost nothing) can distract me from my book, because reading is the best.

But as it turns out, today's Quiet Time was a little different than usual.

Normally we sit at our desks during Quiet

Time, and Ms. Bloom sits at hers and reads too. But today, Ms. Bloom said, "Let's shake things up a little. You've all been so good about Quiet Time that I think you've earned some Special Privileges. Who wants to sit in the hangout corner today while we read?" We all raised our hands, because the hangout corner is fun, and there are colorful chairs that are soft and comfortable. "Maggie, Ben, and Sasha," Ms. Bloom said. "Now, who wants to sit on the beanbag chairs?"

This was an even better treat, because the beanbag chairs are squishy and GREAT, plus there are only two of them in the other corner of the classroom, so everyone raised their hands even more. "Cilla," Ms. Bloom said, "and . . . Colleen." She clapped her hands quickly. "All right, everyone, grab your books and let's go—quiet time starts in five, four, three . . ."

So I grabbed my book and raced to the beanbag chairs. I didn't even have time to be nervous because I'd be with Colleen, or to be surprised, because Ms. Bloom usually keeps us far apart at times like this because we do something called "losing focus."

Quiet Time began. I sank into my beanbag chair and tried to concentrate on my book. But I couldn't. I looked over at Colleen, in the beanbag chair right next to me. She wasn't reading either. But she wasn't looking at me. She was just looking down at the floor.

I turned away quickly. Colleen was probably upset that she had to sit next to me, because she didn't want to be my friend anymore. I decided that I was definitely moving to Alaska.

But something made me look back. Because Colleen wasn't looking down in an angry way, I realized suddenly. She wasn't looking down like she didn't want to talk to me. Colleen was looking down, and looking sad. Colleen was looking like she didn't know what to say.

Colleen was being *shy*.

I took a deep breath. And then I called out, in

my quietest whisper. "Colleen," I said, trying not to move my mouth, because this was Quiet Time after all. "I'm sorry," I whispered. "I'm sorry about your grandma, and I'm sorry I didn't say it yesterday. And I didn't mean to only talk about The Blob."

"No," Colleen whispered back, finally looking up. "*I'm* sorry. I didn't mean those things, and my mom says it was because I was upset, but that still isn't a reason to be mean to someone else. I felt AWFUL for what I said."

I could feel my eyes getting funny again. And I didn't want to be a baby, but when I looked at Colleen, she was blinking very fast, and this made *me* blink very fast, and then she sniffled and then *I* sniffled.

"Cilla!" she said.

"Colleen!" I said.

And then we were hugging each other across our beanbag chairs, and I tried not to but I might have sort of wiped my nose on her shirt.

And the funniest part is, Ms. Bloom didn't even get mad, even though we were DEFINITELY not using our Privileges responsibly and *everyone* was looking at us. Ms. Bloom just walked over, still reading her book, and put a box of tissues down between us. Then she walked back to her desk and sat back down.

**That afternoon, at recess, Colleen and I ran** out to play.

"What did you do at recess yesterday?" Colleen asked.

"I wrote in my book," I said.

"What story?"

I told her about what I'd written so far.

"How does it end?" she asked.

I giggled.

"You know," I said.

"Tell me again," Colleen said, bouncing up and down, and clapping her hands together. "I LOVE this story."

So I did.

And now that I'm home, lying on my mom's fuzzy rug (I tried her desk, but it was too big for me), I'll tell you.

First, let me set the scene.

Setting the scene is a very important thing to do when you're a writer. It gives your reader an idea of what it was like to be somewhere during an exciting or interesting time. So imagine, reader, that all your classmates are sitting around Ms. Cotton on the day she's going to read from your class book.

Ms. Cotton says, "Are you excited, everyone? We're going to see how the story turns out, and even *I* haven't seen the whole thing." And you nod your head, along with everyone else, and you're very excited, though maybe a little nervous too, because your work is going to be read aloud to the *whole class*.

"'Once upon a time,'" Ms. Cotton begins, "'there was a cat.'" (Ms. Cotton drew the first page in the story, and there's an orange cat underneath a smiling sun, confirming your suspicions about

87

her imagination. Specifically, that she doesn't have one.)

" 'The cat liked flowers, and picked some for her family.' " (Annie Abbott's page has a white cat with pink flowers in its paws.)

" 'Then the cat drew a picture to go with the flowers, and put it in a frame.' " (Nick Anderson, brown cat and a box of crayons.)

" 'It was very pretty, and the cat gave the picture to her mom and she smiled.' " (Sally Bell, white cat wearing yellow slippers, which I liked.)

And it goes like that, all the way to: " 'And then the cat had some milk, because she was thirsty.' " (Billy Lane, of course.)

Imagine holding your breath then as the page flips to a page you know well, because it's *your* page. And your first-ever public reading has begun.

" 'And then,' " Ms. Cotton continues, then pauses, surprised, because the page has changed, and it's covered with Ms. Lynn's pretty cursive handwriting.

"'And then the cat found a rocket ship, and went to have tea with the magical princess of the moon, and ate cakes and chocolate cream puffs. And they had a great time, and the magical princess of the moon gave the kitten moondust as a present. The cat was tired from all her travels, so when she got home, she took a nap in her bed, which was made of the finest satin woven by fairy princesses, and had been given to her as a gift by the friendly troll Znod, though that's a story for another time.'"

And the picture along with the story is of the princess of the moon, pouring tea for the kitten next to her magical moon throne with the rocket ship waiting nearby. And underneath it all, in big letters, it says "A page by CILLA Lee-Jenkins."

Ms. Cotton turns the page. "Um, then." She clears her throat. "'Then the kitten woke up and decided to go for a walk.'" (Michael Lerner, purple cat, in a park.)

A page by CILLA
Lee-Jenkins

And then the most amazing thing happens.

"Was that *your* page?" a girl sitting close by leans toward you, whispering excitedly.

"Yes," you whisper back nervously.

"*WOW*," the girl says with a big smile. "I want to visit the magical princess of the moon!"

"I'm Cilla," you say to your first-ever fan.

"I'm Colleen," she says back. And for the first time, you're glad to be in kindergarten.

* * *

**After story time, Ms. Lynn came up to me and** said, "Great story!" And Ms. Cotton said, "What an imagination, Cilla."

So I smiled and said, "Yes. Thank you."

Colleen and I went to recess together and sat on the swings, and I told her more about the magical princess of the moon, and she told me about her imaginary friend named Sheffield, who is a giant pink canary.

And I knew then that I'd found a best friend.

After that day, I had someone to sit with at snack time, and to play with on the playground. Colleen introduced me to Rosa and Sally. I even played with Sophie, and she wasn't so bad any-more, now that I had Colleen to be my friend.

I liked kindergarten after that. As it turns out, you can learn a lot there. I learned that you don't have to play kickball at recess, especially when a best friend is there to help you build little houses for the fairies you've imagined (and who you're sure will come and live in them after dark). When you find a big stick buried in the dirt and want to pretend it's a dinosaur bone and that you've just made the scientific discovery of a lifetime, your best friend will pretend along with you, even though you both know it's probably just a stick. Your best friend will play with you on the bus, and you'll pretend your hands are dinosaurs and put on a show for only yourselves and laugh so hard that it takes you a minute to realize the

whole bus is looking at you. But your best friend won't care.

And as I explained to my dad when I got off the bus today and he asked me how it had gone with Colleen, it turns out that when there's a best friend involved, trouble with words isn't all that big a deal. Because your best friend knows that there's more to you than the words you accidentally say, or don't say. And you know the same thing about her.

So when you're feeling shy and quiet, or are just sitting there happy that she's there too, like I was today, your best friend will sit with you, and it's okay to feel like not saying anything.

Though this doesn't happen much, I've found. Because when there's a best friend involved, there are always things to talk about, and more than enough words to go around.

And I should know.

Words are my life's work, after all.

# QUESTIONS

Right now it's spring break, which is when you get a week off from school and Ms. Bloom goes to Aruba. Colleen's away too, though not in Aruba. She's visiting her grandma and grandpa, and she's going to be her grandma's Special Helper while she gets better.

My spring break has been good. Colleen slept over at my house before she left, and we baked cookies and played in the yard and had an AMAZING time. I was happy that my mom suggested Colleen come over here, because the last time I had a sleepover at her house, it didn't go so well. Specifically, I got scared and my dad had to come and take me home.

I've been spending a lot of time with my mom and dad, and with my Nai Nai and Ye Ye and Grandma and Grandpa Jenkins. In fact, yesterday, I got to go to work with Grandpa Jenkins, which is always A LOT of fun.

My Grandpa Jenkins is a lawyer, and he says I'll be a lawyer too when I grow up. This is because I ask lots of questions, such as, why is your hair disappearing? Or, what's antifungal cream and why is it in your bathroom?

Grandpa Jenkins also says I'm an excellent bargainer. For example, when my grandpa takes me to the toy store for a special treat and tells me I can get *one* thing, I sometimes say, "Look, I'll tell you what. How about if I get the teddy bear *and* the stegosaurus, but not the sparkly cow stickers? Does that work for you?"

Even though this never actually works (and didn't work when it came to The Blob), my Grandpa Jenkins always says, "Golly, the kid is perfect lawyer material." ("Golly" is the Jenkins way of saying "wow!" or "really!" or "ay yah!")

I went to work with Grandpa Jenkins because my mom and dad had to go to the doctor's for the day. (Babies in stomachs need to be checked out A LOT, which isn't fair, because The Blob isn't even born yet, so I don't see why my mom and dad need to spend SO MUCH time with it.) I spent the night before with my Nai Nai and Ye Ye, because my parents had to leave early for The Blob's appointment. It was great, and Nai Nai cooked sausage in rice, which is delicious.

The next morning, Nai Nai drove me to my grandma and grandpa's house and we sang in the car like we always do. Then I got to ride the *train* with Grandpa Jenkins, which is VERY exciting because I'm allowed to stand up as long as I hold on to the pole with both hands.

Grandpa Jenkins works in a tall, tall building with big windows, two elevators, and a man named Harold who always opens the door for us and says, "Silly Lee, give me five!" And I do, even though that's *not* my name, because Harold is nice.

Lawyers sit in big offices and move paper around on their desks all day. My Grandpa Jenkins is especially good at this, and also at being on the telephone and saying, "Don, I'll level with you. Fifty thousand, take it or leave it." Grandpa Jenkins is the best lawyer out there—he told me so.

When he goes to work, my grandpa wears a dark gray suit with a bow tie instead of a regular tie. He always has a handkerchief in his pocket, and the handkerchief has his initials on it, which he puts there himself because he likes to do something called "embroidery" while he watches cowboy movies at night. On the way to work he wears a straw hat with a dip at the top and a black band around it. My grandma calls him "dapper," my mom calls him "spiffy," and my dad calls him "hilarious."

After I sat in Grandpa Jenkins's office all morning and drew new pictures for his walls (I'm his official decorator), we went to lunch. This is another big thing with lawyers. I had a grilled cheese sandwich with crispy, curly French fries, and when we were done we split a piece of cake on the condition that he won't tell my mom and I won't tell my grandma.

We went back to his office after lunch, and while he moved some more papers around, I spent some time with his secretary named Pam, who's very nice and calls me "a treasure." Pam's desk is outside in the lobby, right next to a giant fish tank that's fun to sit by. Pam wears very high heels, which is exciting because I love high heels. They make you tall, and you can use them to make homes for worms in your backyard. Also, when you hook high heels on your ears, they stay on. Unfortunately, I will never, ever, "Do you hear me, Young Lady?," ever be allowed to wear high heels of my own until I'm twenty-five, which is my punishment for the time I accidentally used my mom's special Prada heels to dig in the dirt. And then I got mud all over the rug when I came inside the house because the shoes were on my ears and the dirt kept falling and I didn't realize it. My mom was Not Happy, to say the least.

*Anyway*, yesterday Pam let me help her bring around coffee and tea to the lawyers in the office. Which brings me back to questions. Because lawyers, as I've mentioned before, ask a lot of them.

Yesterday, when I went around visiting with the coffee, *everyone* wanted to know:

1. How are you?
2. Would you like some candy?
3. How's school?
4. What grade are you in?
5. Wait, really? They grow up so fast! And that makes you how old?
6. Wow. Time flies when you get old, Cilla, did you know that?

Usually, the questions are the same. But today, there was a lawyer there who I hadn't met before, though Pam said he had been at the firm for a long time. His name is Mr. Lewis, and he was very nice and has hair that's silver like the pieces of hair my Grandpa Jenkins has just on the sides of his head.

Mr. Lewis offered me candy from the bowl on his desk. And he asked me a *new* question.

"Lee-Jenkins?" he said. "Quite a special heritage."

"Thank you," I said. (Because being special is always a good thing, so it was definitely a compliment.)

"So," he went on, smiling. "Where are you from?"

I had to think about this for a minute. I'm supposed to be on my Best Behavior at my Grandpa Jenkins's office, which mostly means saying "please" and "thank you" a lot, but which also means that I need to give polite, grown-up answers to questions, even if I don't quite understand what they're asking. But I figured it out, and told him my address.

"Er, yes," he said, offering me another piece of candy, which I took again, because even though it wasn't chocolate, peppermint is still delicious. "I mean, where are you from originally?"

"Um." I had to think about this. I knew there was something he wanted to know, but I didn't think I understood the question.

So I decided to give him the most honest answer.

"My mom's stomach," I said.

I think this was an okay answer, because he didn't ask anything else after that. He just said, "Oh," and looked surprised (which was strange, because I'm pretty sure most adults are supposed to know all about babies and stomachs).

"Come on, Cilla," Pam poked her head into the office, and she must have just heard a funny joke, because she was trying not to laugh. "Your grandpa's looking for you, and Mr. Lewis probably needs to get back to work."

"Okay," I said. "Bye, Mr. Lewis. Thank you for the candy." (I'm excellent at Best Behavior.)

"Erm, you're welcome," he said. He still looked confused, but I figured he'd catch up, eventually.

It's funny, because even though Mr. Lewis didn't ask me as many questions as everyone else, I was still thinking about his question later in the day, when we were getting ready to go.

I had just finished saying goodbye to Pam and the fish when my grandpa said, "You're looking thoughtful, Cilla dear. Everything all right?"

"Yes," I said, as we stepped into the elevator. And it was, mostly.

"Lawyers really *do* ask a lot of questions, don't they?" I asked, after the elevator doors had closed behind us.

"Golly, Cilla." He laughed. "You're absolutely right. It's exhausting, isn't it?"

"Yes," I said. "I don't know how they get all their work done and lunches eaten with all the time they spend on questions. Golly and ay yah!"

Maybe I'll look into being a lawyer as a backup job if I ever want a break from bestselling writing. I know it would make my grandpa happy. But I don't think it will happen. Even though I like knowing things, I don't think I like questions as much as lawyers do, no matter what Grandpa Jenkins says.

And even though Mr. Lewis said nice things about me, I still didn't like his question. Because this has happened to me before. I get asked questions A LOT, like "Where are you from?" and "What are you?" (which is the only one I have a good answer to). I used to think these questions were because people could tell I was special (which I am, of course, because Destiny). But now, I'm not so sure if this kind of special is a good thing to be.

I wonder why people need to know these things. I wonder why they're always so surprised to know the answers.

And I wonder if *I'm* doing something wrong that makes them need to ask.


**Yesterday, when I got home from my grandpa's** office, my mom and I cuddled on the couch, and I looked at her stomach for a long time. I thought about how everyone will know who I am someday, because I'll be famous. So no one will need to ask me questions about my family anymore, or what I am, or where I'm from. They'll just know.

But they won't know about The Blob. Because The Blob will be a normal, not-famous baby. And I wonder if The Blob will be asked where *it's* from.

And I wonder what its answer will be, and will people be able to tell that we're sisters, or will they have to ask about that, too?

I put my ear on my mom's stomach and listened. I almost patted it, and I almost asked if it

would kick this much when it came out of her stomach, and if it was maybe a secret ninja (which would be GREAT). But then I remembered I'm not excited for it to come.

I didn't talk about Mr. Lewis either, because my parents were smiling and happy. They put on music and danced, and my dad showed me something he calls the tango but my mom calls "embarrassing yourself" (but then she did it too, and seemed to be having a great time, so it can't be that bad).

And I didn't want to make them sad.

So I didn't ask my questions. I'm not brave, or a lawyer. And sometimes, I even think that I don't want to know the answers at all.

So I guess I never will.

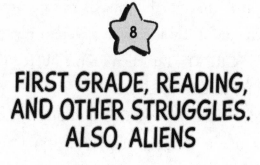

# FIRST GRADE, READING, AND OTHER STRUGGLES. ALSO, ALIENS

**Tonight my mom read to me from** *Selena Moon and the Moonstone*, which is my favorite book. It's about a girl named Selena Moon who's brave, and smart, and finds out that she can change the color of the sky with the powers of her mind. She and her best friend, Colin, and his pet chimera, Evelyn, have adventures together, and they foil the plans of the evil Sorcerer Lord, though he promises revenge (as evil Sorcerer Lords do). This is important in the second book, *Selena Moon and the Prophecy of the Waxing Crescent*, because Colin is kidnapped by the Sorcerer Lord, and Selena and Evelyn have to find him before it's too late! There's A LOT of Suspense and drama. Also dragon fire. And car chases.

My copy of *Selena Moon* has cracks on its cover and side. Its pages are wavy and soft at the edges, and some of them are a little wrinkled. This is because I read *Selena Moon* ALL THE TIME. I even keep it on my bedside table, and sometimes in my bed, just because I like to have it near me. And when I want to reread my favorite scene, or a moment when a character said something funny, or did something GREAT, I like to have it by me so I can open it right away.

Even though I can read *Selena Moon* by myself (of course), I still like it when my mom reads it to me, too. She does GREAT voices for all the characters. And The Blob kicked when my mom read, which means it at least has good taste in books.

Before she said

good night, my mom asked me to write a story for her to read when she's in the hospital, so she'll have something from me close by. I like that idea, even if I don't like the reason she'll be there. I decided that my story would be about a penguin. But I changed my mind later and decided it would be about a moose, and then an elephant, and then maybe a toucan. There are so many options.

My mom also said that she's sorry she's been so tired lately. Her stomach is getting REALLY big now, and sometimes when she walks, she waddles like a duck. (Apparently, this is an opinion I should keep to myself. I know this because I didn't, and then I got in trouble, and then my dad laughed and he got in trouble.)

But even though I *was* disappointed, and kind of mad, when we couldn't go to the park yesterday because she needed to lie down, I said, "It's okay, Mommy. I understand." And my mom smiled and gave me a hug and said she loved me very much. Which was nice.

Now I'm in bed, but I don't feel like reading anymore. And it's funny, because even though I love *Selena Moon* more than any other book in the whole world, lying here next to it reminds me of a time when it didn't always make me feel that great. In fact, there was a time when I'd look at my copy of *Selena Moon* and feel really, really bad, even though it was my favorite book. Which is a confusing way to feel.

This is a story I don't talk about much, because it has a lot of Struggles and some bad feelings in it. But there are good parts too, and it's an important story if you really want to know who the real Cilla (or Eliadora, or Panzanella) was as a child.

Let me set the scene:

It was the first day of first grade. Mr. Ogden introduced himself, and we played a game where we said our names and shared two funny things that describe us. We had to sit in alphabetical order, which meant I wasn't next to Colleen, but we were close enough that we could make silly faces at each other from across the aisle. And then Mr. Ogden wrote a few sentences on the board and asked everyone to copy them so he could see us practice our handwriting.

And suddenly, even though I was in a class with Colleen and Tims #1 and #2 and Valerie and lots of people I knew and liked, I didn't feel like a part of them anymore (not even Colleen—my BEST friend!). Because they all looked at the board, and I knew that instead of letters they saw words, and maybe even instead of words, they saw a sentence, and instead of a sentence, maybe even a *story*.

But I didn't.

I couldn't.

Because I had a secret.

I, Cilla Lee-Jenkins, future author extraordinaire, didn't know how to read.

I don't know why I had this problem. And I don't know how it even happened. But sometime over summer break, Colleen had started reading parts of *Selena Moon* on her own, and now suddenly, all the other kids could read too. And even though I wanted to read more than ANYTHING, and even though I'd practiced every day over the summer with my mom and dad, I still couldn't do it.

On that day in first grade, all I could do was look at the board and draw shapes. My face was hot, and every new line I drew with my pencil made my stomach feel tight, because what if I was copying a smudge instead of a part of an actual letter? And how was I supposed to know the difference, and how did everyone else already know the difference?

That night, after my parents finished reading to me and kissed me good night, I opened my copy of *Selena Moon*. I looked hard at the pages and I decided to MAKE them make sense to me. But all I saw were letters, and I knew there were rules about the sounds they made, but I couldn't remember what they were. And this made me sad again, but it also made me angry, and I threw my book—my *Selena Moon!*—away from me. It hit the ground with a loud thud, and I felt TERRIBLE, and I rushed out of bed to make sure it was okay.

This is where my parents found me, because *Selena* made a lot of noise. My dad picked me up, and carried me back to bed, and sat with me until I stopped crying. And when he asked me what was the matter, I told him that I would never be an author. Because how can you be destined for literary greatness, or ANYTHING great at all, when you can't even read your favorite book?

It didn't help that as first grade went on, I had to go to a special reading class with Ms. Brown every Tuesday and Thursday, while the rest of the class had reading and snack time. My parents said it would be fun, and that there was nothing wrong with seeing Ms. Brown, and maybe I'd meet some new people and make new friends. But this wasn't helpful, because I wanted to have fun with Colleen

and the friends I already had, the friends who *could*
read. And if there was nothing wrong with it, then
why did we have to leave class while everyone else
stayed behind and did fun projects?

Besides, there was only one other student from Mr. Ogden's class who had to go to Ms. Brown's class too, and I already knew that we were NOT going to be friends. This was because he was an Annoying Individual.

A VERY Annoying Individual.

And his name was Ben McGee.

Here are a few things you should know about Ben McGee, which I noticed during those first weeks of Ms. Brown's class:

1. He was definitely *not* shy. He always talked to the other kids at the table, even though he didn't know them, and even though he was new in school (new kids are always supposed to be quiet and scared—this is a rule).

2. He was very curious, and was always asking questions like "Is

your refrigerator running?" and
"Why?" and "What's up, Silly
Lee?" (The answer to that is
"nothing" because "Silly Lee" is
NOT my name.)

3. He had a hard time concentrating
on work too, which is how he
sometimes noticed me watching
him, and then he would ask me
questions (see above). Or he'd
make faces. (Which were usually
NOT funny. Though sometimes
I'd laugh, because I couldn't help
it, and then we'd get in trouble.)

4. He knew all about the San Diego
Zoo and talked about zoo animals
ALL THE TIME, because his
family had taken a trip there.
And he said that manatees were
boring, even though I love
manatees, even though I've never

seen one, because on the day he
was there the manatee just sat
in its tank.

5. He didn't drink his juice at snack
time. So I drank it for him.
6. He smelled. Somehow, I knew
this. It was in the way he moved.

But the really, really important thing you should know about Ben McGee isn't something you can see right away. I didn't see it at first either. Until one day, when I was getting ready to leave for Ms. Brown's class.

We were all getting our snacks from our cubbies, and from across the room, I heard Colleen and a few other kids laughing.

"What's so funny?" I asked, walking over to them.

"We're writing stories in reading today," Tim #1 said. "And Sasha had a great idea for one."

"Oh," I said. "Will you tell—"

But just then Ms. Brown came, and I had to go.

"Have a good time, Cilla." Colleen waved. "I'll miss you."

That was nice to hear. But then I saw her bounce over to her group, and they all had smiles and laughed again about a story that wasn't mine—a story that *everyone* would get to read.

And I despaired.

Only, when we got to reading, Ben McGee wouldn't let me despair in peace, which was frustrating. We were using little squares with letters on them to make words, which was actually fun, even though I was trying hard not to enjoy myself.

"Hey," he whispered as I sat playing with my squares. "Silly Lee."

"My name is NOT Silly Lee," I said, forgetting to ignore him.

"Oh, right. Silly Lee-*Jenkins*." He grinned.

"You are SO annoying, Ben McGee." I sighed. "Also, that's not original at all." Being original is very important to me.

"Don't care," he said, which I knew he'd say because he's unoriginal, plus that's what he always says when I accuse him of being unoriginal, which is all the time.

"So," he said after another minute, even though I was CLEARLY trying to get back to my game. "Whatcha doing?"

"Nothing," I said, taking a deep breath and trying to sound quiet, because that's what you're supposed to do when things are Tragic. "Just being sad."

"Why?" he asked.

"Because," I said.

"Because why?"

"Why do you ask SO many questions?" I huffed.

"I dunno," he said. "Just because."

I shook my head and went back to my tiles.

"Is it because everyone else gets to write stories today?" he asked, after a minute.

I looked at him, surprised.

"I figured that was it," he went on, "since you're a GIANT book nerd and all."

"You are a pain, Ben McGee," I said hotly, glaring at him.

"I'm just saying what you are," he said. "Besides, *everyone* knows that your story would've been the best, if you'd been able to write one too. So you don't have to get mad—being a book nerd isn't a bad thing."

I didn't know what to say.

"You're a funny boy, Ben McGee," I said, finally.

He shrugged. "Yeah, I know. My mom says that too. She says she doesn't know where I get it from, and it must be my dad's side of the family. But Dad says he doesn't know where I get it from either. He says I might as well have dropped in from outer space. So it's a mystery."

And suddenly, everything changed.


**When I went back to class that day, I ran up** to Colleen.

"Colleen," I said. "You'll *never* guess what happened in reading."

"What?" Colleen asked.

"I found out the most AMAZING thing about Ben McGee," I said. "Ben McGee"—I paused to add drama—"Ben McGee is . . . an alien."

"What?!"

"An alien," I confirmed. "It all makes sense now."

But just then Mr. Ogden told us to sit down for

math, and then Marcy Thompson wanted to sit with us at lunch and wouldn't leave us alone at recess either. In writing, a delay like this is called Suspense, and it's a good thing to have, but in real life it's just called "annoying," especially when Marcy Thompson is involved.

Luckily, Colleen and I got a seat on the bus all to ourselves that afternoon, so I could explain everything.

"You see," I said, picking up where I'd left off, because you can do that with a best friend, "it all makes sense now. He only came to our school in first grade, and his own mother doesn't know where he comes from, and his dad says he's from outer space. Ben McGee is an alien, sent here to gather information about us for his people."

"But why elementary school?" Colleen asked. "Why would he come to Mr. Ogden's class if he wanted to learn about humans? Wouldn't he go somewhere important, with adults? Like the post office."

"Or the gas station," I added, realizing she

was right. "Unless . . . That's it! Unless he made a mistake! Unless he didn't know what humans look like, and when he came here, he got confused and didn't take on the right kind of disguise."

Colleen was with me now.

"He's super good at math," she said, leaning in excitedly.

"He knew all the answers in our lesson on animals that live in the desert today," I added.

"He doesn't know that new students are supposed to be shy and scared."

"The way he loves animals and talks about the zoo ALL the time."

"The way he doesn't understand how to call people by their names."

"Ben McGee," I summed up, "is an alien, sent to Earth to study us. But he accidentally landed in the wrong place."

"The desert," Colleen specified, "and saw nothing around but desert animals."

"*Camels*. Which explains why he never drinks his juice."

"Yes," Colleen said, bouncing up and down. "He thought the camels were people, so he turned into one, and only realized his mistake when actual humans came and took him to the zoo."

"And he had to live there until he could escape without being seen, when someone—"

"Mrs. McGee!"

"Yes, Mrs. McGee came too close to the camel cage!"

"And now he's disguised as her son!" Colleen concluded, throwing her hands out wide in excitement.

"His real alien-face lurking behind the human face of the first grader known as Ben McGee"—I threw my hands out too—"waiting to bring information about us back to his people!"

"That," Colleen said, slumping back in her seat, "is the BEST story I've heard *all year*."

# FIRST GRADE, PART II.
# MORE ALIENS,
# AND HALLOWEEN

I enjoyed first grade a little more after that day with Alien-Face McGee. And I was having more fun in reading, because the games we played were great, and Ms. Brown said my reading was improving in something called "leaps and bounds." But I still wanted to read *Selena Moon* more than ANYTHING in the world.

So it was VERY important to me that everything was *perfect* for one of my favorite holidays of all time—Halloween.

Halloween is very special to me. It's all about imagination, after all. I always make my costume, and my mom and dad help, though sometimes they say my costumes need to be something called "actually possible to create." (Like the year I wanted to be a sarcophagus. Though to be fair, my dad didn't say "no" right away. He said, "Hmmm," when I told him about it. But then my mom said, "Nathan," and my dad said, "We have a lot of plywood," and Mom said, "Absolutely not," and Dad said, "We could put it on wheels," and Mom said, "Nathan, please," with her eyebrows raised and a Parent Look in my direction. So I was a dinosaur princess instead.)

I'm also not allowed to start my Halloween costume until September 1, because apparently my parents don't appreciate it when I start making costume sketches in January. But that still gives me LOTS of time to find a costume, and that year in first grade, Colleen and I knew exactly what we wanted to be. We were going to be—who else?— Selena and Colin, from *Selena Moon*, because they were our favorite characters.

Our plans were going perfectly, too. Until, one

day, on the playground, when Colleen had just told me that her dad had an old purple suit jacket that she could wear for her Colin costume, and that her mom had an old cane that I could use for Selena's staff. We were both excited about this news, and jumping up and down, which made the beads Colleen sometimes wears in her hair clack like they were excited too.

"Yay!" I said, because our costumes were going to be the BEST ever.

"Did you say *Selena Moon*?" a voice cut in. Neither of us had noticed Sasha Simpson standing by us, next to the slides. I didn't know her very well. Mostly because I was scared to talk to her, because she had lots of friends, and was really good at telling funny jokes, plus her hair always stayed brushed.

"I love *Selena Moon*!" Sasha exclaimed. "I'm going to be Selena for Halloween too—my mom's already ordered the Deluxe Costume Pack online. It even comes with a temporary sun tattoo, just like Selena's."

"You . . ." I looked at Sasha, surprised. "You like *Selena Moon*?"

"Yeah, that movie was soooooooo cool. Everyone's going to be someone from *Selena Moon* this year—Connor's already ordered his Colin costume, which looks just like the one from the movie. It even has the green jacket. We'll all match!"

"Oh," I said. I wasn't sure how I felt about this.

"That's nice . . . ," Colleen said, hesitating.

"What, you guys haven't seen it?" Sasha said.

"No, we saw it," Colleen said. "And it was okay, but they got a few things wrong. Like Colin's jacket is purple, not green."

"And they cut out some really exciting parts," I said quietly, trying to help Colleen. "Like the story with Selena's mom."

"Oh, I haven't read the books." Sasha laughed. "But I'm a total Selena fan! You two don't like the movie?" She looked confused.

"I did . . ." I wasn't sure what to say. "It's just that it was a book first, before a movie," I tried to explain. "And the books are . . . well, *books*. And the story is so much more exciting when it's in your head."

"I guess." Sasha shrugged. "But between you, me, Erica, Liz, and Sally, we'll have a classroom full of Selenas, and then Colleen, Connor, and the two Tims as Colin. You guys had better order your costumes before they all sell out!" And then she skipped away, back to her friends on the slide, singing, "We're all going to match on Halloween, this will be *so cool*."

Colleen and I watched her go, and I saw Colleen's shoulders droop. Suddenly, my brilliant Halloween costume plan didn't seem so great anymore.

**That night, I was quiet and distracted. In fact,** I was in a state of general artistic despair, and so not paying attention to anything, which my parents realized right around the time my mom mentioned dessert and I didn't even notice.

"Cilla," my mom said, putting down her fork and speaking in her concerned voice. "Is everything okay?"

"No," I mumbled finally.

"What's wrong?" my dad said, putting his fork down, in his concerned voice. "Do you want to talk about it?"

"Yes," I said, putting down my fork, because it seemed to be the thing to do. "Colleen and I *were* going to be Selena Moon characters for Halloween, but . . ." I told them about Sasha and all the other kids, and how this meant that everyone would think that Colleen and I were just regular *Selena Moon* movie fans, instead of special book fans, and everything was AWFUL.

"Um, well, I'm sorry, Cilla," my dad said. "Maybe we can make you a different costume from *Selena Moon*, so you don't look like everyone else."

"No," I said. "It won't be the same. No costume is as good as the real-life book Selena (not the imaginary movie kind). And all the other characters are taken too. I bet even Alien-Face McGee is going to dress up as someone from the *Selena Moon* movie—"

"Priscilla Lee-Jenkins." My mom cut me off, and not in a Changing the Subject kind of way. I could tell she was Not Happy. "What have I told you about calling people names?"

"It's not a mean name, plus I haven't actually called him that," I pointed out reasonably. "It's just a story I made up."

"Cilla." My mom sighed, and ran her hands through her hair. "It might be just a story to you, but you still can't call people names."

"But the creature calling itself Ben McGee—" I began. Mom glared. "Ben McGee," I corrected myself, "calls me names too. He calls me Silly Lee-Jenkins and a GIANT book nerd—" I stopped short.

"Well, you're right," my mom admitted. "It's not nice of him to say those things. But that doesn't mean . . ." She went on.

But I wasn't listening anymore.

Suddenly, I'd had an idea.

* * *

**On Halloween, my favorite night of the year,** the moon was full and round, and the sky was dark with wisps of black clouds at its edges. The leaves were crispy and red, and the jack-o'-lanterns on our neighbors' porches shone yellow and orange in the dark. This was perfect for creating Mood and Atmosphere, which are both very important in stories. It felt like Halloween, but without being too scary, which is also very important in my opinion.

I'd promised my mom that I wouldn't call Alien-Face McGee names, or tell anyone at school my story about him, and I'd mostly kept that promise. I only talked about it with Colleen, who already knew, and maybe Sally. And Colleen had thought it was such a good story that she'd told Valerie. And Tim #2. And #1. But that's it.

One thing I'd definitely not told anyone about, though, was my Halloween costume. Colleen and I had made a solemn pinky-swear-promise not to say what we were going to be.

On Halloween, my street was full of kids in costumes. There were some witches and ghosts, but mostly, there were Selenas and Colins. Colleen and I walked side by side, our parents not too far behind. I was People Watching. So it didn't take me long to spot Sasha, Connor, the Tims, and a whole group of kids from Mr. Ogden's first-grade class, all trick-or-treating. Colleen and I smiled at each other nervously, and then began to wave.

Sasha and Connor and the Tims, all in the costumes their moms had bought them, saw us. Each of us wore a giant cardboard box, which my dad had helped us cut so there was one big hole at the top for our heads, and two small holes at the sides for our arms. On the front, back, and each side were exact copies of the cover and spine of *Selena Moon and the Moonstone* for me, and *Selena Moon and the Prophecy of the Waxing Crescent* for Colleen, which we had spent the entire month of October painting in my garage, with my parents helping us with the writing parts. Because we were the Selena Moon books for Halloween.

"Whoa," Sasha said. "You guys look amazing!"

"Thanks," I said, smiling. Sasha was wearing her Selena Moon Deluxe Costume Pack, but I noticed that she'd added to it too, with a belt that was painted with glitter glue and had *all* the star and moon symbols that were on Selena's real belt, in the book *and* in the movie. And I realized that Sasha was really and truly a *Selena Moon* fan too. (Though nothing can ever be quite as good as the Selena Moon books. They're bestsellers, after all.)

"You look great too, Selena," I said, which made Sasha smile even wider.

"That must have taken forever," Connor said, examining Colleen's costume.

"There's writing on the back, too," Colleen said proudly, turning around so he could see. "Also, I'm wearing purple, because I'm a Colin-themed book."

"And I'm a Selena-themed book." I grinned.

"This is great," Sasha exclaimed. "Cilla and Colleen are our mascots—the biggest fans of all!"

"Hooray for *Selena Moon*!" Colleen cheered. (She always knows just what to say.)

"Let's go trick-or-treating!" one of the Tims yelled. And we all said "yay!" and set off as a group, the *Selena Moon* book and movie fans.

I'd fallen behind Colleen, because I needed to readjust my cardboard box, when I heard someone next to me say, "Nice."

I turned. There was a boy in an animal mask, with a backpack stuffed under an old sweater to give him a hump.

"Do you like it?" The unmistakable voice of Ben McGee came from behind the mask. "Camels are my favorite animal. I always ask my mom to take me to see them when we go to the zoo."

"It's . . . very nice," I said, trying to hide my reaction, since I'd made a promise to my mom and all.

"Yours is okay," Ben McGee said, gesturing to

my costume. I opened my mouth to say something back, because I was sure he was making fun of me, but he kept going before I could think of anything good.

"But Book Two is my favorite. When Selena and Evelyn have to work together to stop the witch's prophecy? Best chapter ever."

Slowly, I closed my mouth.

"You like the Selena Moon books?" I looked at him suspiciously, expecting him to laugh and say "Just kidding, Silly."

"They're my favorites," he said. "My mom reads them to me every night."

I didn't know what to say. So finally I just said, "Thank you, Ben McGee. You gave me the idea. With the whole book nerd thing."

The camel head tilted to the side, thinking.

"Cool," he said. "I'd never think to make a book costume, though, and I love books and stories. Someone told me a story the other day, too, about how I was an alien from outer space who turned into an animal and then went to the zoo before finally becoming me. Have you heard it?"

"I . . . ," I said, looking around to see if my mom was close enough to hear. She wasn't.

And I was surprised, because suddenly I felt kind of bad. I didn't want to hurt Ben McGee's feelings.

"I . . ." There was no way around it. "I might have been the person who made it up," I admitted finally, afraid to look at him.

"Wait, really?!" He pushed up his mask, and he was *smiling*. "This is awesome—no one's ever made up a story about *me* before. What kind of animal was I, after the alien and before first grade?"

"You'll never guess." I smiled back. "I swear, I didn't know camels were your favorite animal," I explained. "When I made the story up, it just came to me when I put all the evidence together."

We walked off, just behind the others—me, Cilla Lee-Jenkins, *Selena Moon and the Moonstone*, and Ben McGee, alien and camel—as I told him his story.

At the end of the evening, as our moms were getting ready to take us home and I was already counting how many chocolate bars I'd gotten in my head, he said, "Bye, Silly Lee! Happy Halloween!"

And I didn't even get mad. I just said, "Happy Halloween to you too, Alien-Face McGee!"


**It wasn't long after Halloween that I opened** *Selena Moon* one day and didn't see letters or *T* and *H* rules, or even sentences. I opened it up and I saw a *story*.

My mom, dad, and Mr. Ogden called it "developmental," which they said means that my brain was growing, and one day it was ready to read. So I guess this part of the story doesn't really have a middle (which all good stories should have—it's usually the part where the hero is slowly getting better at something, like sword fighting or dragon taming, or reading). In a movie, there'd be music playing while this happened, and then at the end everyone would celebrate, and maybe there'd be fireworks. Or trumpets.

But as it turns out, when you've spent seven years of your life wanting to learn to read more than anything else in the whole world, once you learn, there's just SO MUCH to catch up on that you don't even think about asking for fireworks. You're too busy reading.

Sometimes, when I'm lying in bed, and looking at *Selena Moon*, I trace the lines and wrinkles that I made that night when I got so mad that I threw my book away from me.

My mom offered to buy me a new copy, but I didn't want one. Because even though they were made because of Struggles, I don't mind those marks anymore. In fact, sometimes I look at them and imagine that someday, if I'm really lucky, and Destiny was really and truly right that day by the gumball machine, maybe my book will be the first book where the letters come together for someone. Maybe my book will be the first book someone ever reads.


**Alien-Face McGee caught up soon too. And** when he couldn't quite finish a book, or if it was feeling too hard, I'd act the end out for him (or make up an ending, if I hadn't read the book).

As a good writer should.

# COLORS

**The school year's almost over now, which is** sad, because I LOVE Ms. Bloom.

And school is REALLY fun, which is why I haven't been writing much lately. But then yesterday, I looked at my mom's stomach and realized how much The Blob's been growing. So I know I need to hurry to get this book done in time.

Ms. Bloom keeps asking us to reflect on what we've learned this year, which is easy because we've learned so much—the water cycle, multiplication, how to write an acrostic poem, and how to line up (almost) quietly. And this isn't all I've learned. From my mom I learned how to bake chocolate chip cookies, and my dad's taught me to change a lightbulb (you do this by being very careful, and always keeping hold of the ladder with one hand and foot, and asking an adult's permission. Also, there's a little glass bulb involved, but this seems less important than everything else.). From my Grandma Jenkins I learned how to tell the difference between azaleas and rhododendrons, and my Grandpa Jenkins taught me how to make an embroidery cross-stitch. From my Ye Ye I learned how to measure wood before an adult cuts it to make a shelf, and from my Nai Nai I learned that when moms grow babies in their stomachs, they should eat rice cooked in ginger ALL THE TIME.

My mom hates this, but she tells my dad that Nai Nai needs to feel like she's part of the process, and besides, you can't teach an old dog new tricks. I don't know what dogs have to do with it, but I was excited when my mom said this because maybe it means we're getting a pet (though I'd prefer a puppy, actually. I want to teach it tricks. Especially juggling.).

*Anyway*, all these things have been fun to learn.

But none of them are quite as important as the one big, big thing I learned last week. And this had to do with pictures.

It all began when Ms. Bloom told us we were going to paint family portraits and then put our pictures up all over the classroom for everyone to see at our end-of-the-year party. This way, we would finish the year by celebrating who we are and the people who support us. Ms. Bloom says a picture is worth a thousand words, which, as a future best-selling author, sounds HIGHLY suspicious to me.

But at first, the project was exciting. I love family portraits, and I already knew that mine would have everyone in it—my Grandma and Grandpa Jenkins, Nai Nai, Ye Ye, Mom, Dad, and the garden gnome Mrs. Tibbs gave us because her daughter-in-law had given it to her, which meant she couldn't throw it away. My mom wasn't sure if she could accept it when Mrs. Tibbs told us all this, but luckily I was there to say "yes!"

Mrs. Tibbs said, "I knew I could count on you, Cilla," holding the gnome out to my mom.

And my mom said, "Yes. That's our Cilla," in a little voice that wasn't supposed to sound like a sigh but did, and she took the gnome with both hands. (Horatio—which is what I named the gnome—is very heavy, I found out later, when I tried to bring him inside for a tea party and dropped him on the new umbrella stand. Don't worry, he was okay. The umbrella stand, not so much.)

Horatio had a spot of honor in my picture. Also a red hat. This was very convenient, because Ms. Bloom told us to use at least six colors in our pictures, three regular ones and three that we'd mixed.

"Think about your colors," she said. "And when you go home this weekend, take a careful look at the people and things around you. What you think of as just brown hair may be light brown with streaks of red. What you imagine as blue eyes may be blue-green. Color is all around us, and it's a lot more complicated than we think."

Now, at first, I didn't really see what Ms. Bloom meant. I love colors, and am very good at picking them out, because I have Creative Talents. I know this because my mom said she desperately needed my Creative Talents to help her choose what the baby will wear when she comes home. I picked some excellent clothes, and I'll admit that it was *a little* fun (especially when I found a pair of purple pajamas with blue polka dots, yellow socks with orange polka dots, and a green hat with red polka dots and DINOSAURS on it, which was GREAT).

So when I started my picture, the colors seemed easy. I used red for Horatio's hat, then mixed it with white to make pink for his face.

My other colors, though, got a bit trickier.

For my Grandma and Grandpa Jenkins I used gray for their hair (though Grandpa Jenkins doesn't have much), pink for their faces, and blue for their eyes.

The colors for my Nai Nai and Ye Ye were harder to figure out, but I finally found a light peach for their faces and dark brown for their eyes. I found a dark gray for Ye Ye's thick hair, and black for my Nai Nai's.

Then came my mom and dad, and of course, me.

My parents were easy, now that my grand-parents were figured out. My mom had both her parents' pink skin and blue eyes. And, after a looong moment, I decided to give her a very, very small bump in her stomach for the baby, whose name I won't say—small enough that you wouldn't notice it if you didn't know it was there (though that's not what it looks like in real life, because it's getting REALLY big).

My dad had Nai Nai and Ye Ye's peach skin and dark brown eyes, and his hair was black and straight like theirs. I gave my mom and dad match-ing red shirts because they like to tell me they're a team, but sometimes my dad tells my mom that she needs to be more of a team player so I don't think they have it totally figured out yet. I thought maybe the matching shirts would help.

And then there was me. Priscilla. Lee-Jenkins.

I've painted lots of pictures of myself before and they weren't hard. But I'd spent so much time thinking about colors that I suddenly began to notice things I'd never thought about before. Like how my skin isn't like my parents'. It's darker than my mom's but a different color than my dad's—not pink, not peach. My hair isn't black, but it's a dark, dark brown. In the end, none of the colors I used to draw me were the same colors I'd used for the rest of my family.

We hung our pictures on the wall when we were done, and then we had free time and got to look at everyone else's portraits.

Colleen had painted her mom, her dad, and her two brothers, plus her pet goldfish. It was a great picture, and Ms. Bloom said, "You captured the family resemblance so well!"

From Alien-Face McGee's picture, I found out that he has a little sister and two cats along with his parents. Colleen said she liked mine, and Alien-Face wanted to know all about Horatio, which was a fun story to tell. But something didn't feel right.

I didn't know what it was until Colleen looked at my picture and said, "I like your drawing, Cilla. They're all really far apart, though."

And she was right, I saw suddenly. All the other families had been drawn standing together—holding hands, smiling at each other, some even playing games. In my picture, I stood in the middle with my mom, dad, and The Blob. My Grandpa and Grandma Jenkins stood next to us, off to one side, and my Nai Nai and Ye Ye stood on the other side, the whole page in between them.

"It's no big deal," Colleen said.

But it was.

That day, when I got home from school, I went to look at my mom and dad's wedding photo, which they keep on a shelf above the couch. Mostly, I like this photo. My mom and dad are younger than I ever thought they could be, and my mom's hair is long and curls at the end, and her dress is like a real live fairy princess's with white lace and a skirt that poufs and goes all the way to the floor. This is the first photo, my mom says, of her and my dad as a married couple. But it's also special for another reason that we don't talk about. Because it's the only photo ever taken with all of my grandparents in it.

In the photo, my mom and dad are in the center, holding hands. Grandma and Grandpa Jenkins are standing side by side next to my mom. And at the opposite end of the picture, my Nai Nai and Ye Ye are standing next to my dad. Everyone's dressed up, and everyone's smiling.

Except . . . I know better. That smile isn't my

Grandpa Jenkins's smile when he gets a big piece of chocolate cake, or my Grandma Jenkins's when she claps for me in the school play. It's not my Nai Nai's smile when I read her a story, and it's not my Ye Ye's when I find him the perfect tie.

In this picture, my grandparents are pretending.

And real families don't look like that. Real families don't have grandparents who stand as far away from each other as possible, in photos and when you draw them. Real families don't have Nai Nais who say things like "I have errands" when she drops you off at your grandma and grandpa's and you suggest that she come in to say hi. Real families don't have grandmas who say, "Oh, I don't think your Nee Nee, or Nay Nay, or however you say it, would want to hear from me, dear," when you suggest that they get together for lunch, because they both love cookies and tea and pretty plates. Real families don't have grandpas who say, "Your Ye Ye reads you stories too?" in a surprised voice, and then, "Golly, I just never imagined that," which makes no sense because OF COURSE Ye Ye reads me stories—he loves them almost as much as I do. And real families don't have Ye Yes who sometimes forget to speak in English when he's talking to your parents. Or moms who have to smile and pretend her feelings aren't hurt when he does.

They all came to the wedding. It took a lot of convincing, I once heard my dad tell a friend, when he thought I wasn't listening. But in the end, my grandparents wanted my parents to be happy.

But that doesn't change the fact that the only other time my grandparents were ever together after that, and the only time when we were really *all* together, was that day in the hospital, when my parents piled all those names on me. Priscilla. Lee and Jenkins. All those family names on one tiny baby, and all in a family that didn't even want to be a family. And they didn't even take a picture.

And now my mom and dad are going to have another baby. A regular blob baby, not a genius like me. A baby who's going to have even more names stuck on her.

And *I'll* be the only other person who really

understands what it's like to be a Lee-Jenkins, and having Big Sister Responsibilities means that *I'll* be the one who has to protect my little sister from the Rude Individuals and Tough Crowds and Cousin Helens and Mr. Lewises.

So the picture I drew isn't worth a thousand words. Because I don't think this can be done, no matter how many words you use.

**That Saturday, I went to spend the afternoon** with my Grandma Jenkins. We were sitting in the kitchen, rolling out cookie dough, and I thought about Ms. Bloom, and how the colors on my grandma's hands weren't just pink, but were all sorts of things. There were red spots and white spots and pink and dots of blue. There were so many colors, and none of them were the same as the colors on my skin.

"Grandma," I said suddenly. "Do you mind that I'm not like you?"

She paused mid-roll and turned to me with a

funny expression. "Why, what do you mean, Priscilla dear?"

"I'm your granddaughter," I said, trying to explain, "and I'm not like you."

"Why, Cilla," she said, smiling. "You're so much like me."

I paused, and looked at her like I didn't believe her. But she just laughed.

"Want to know a secret?" she asked.

"Yes," I said, not sure how this was an answer to my question. But I love secrets, I can't lie.

Grandma Jenkins leaned in close.

"Your mom told me about the gnome and the umbrella stand. When I was little, I wanted to play imaginary games with the paperweight shaped like a crane that my mother, who you are named for, kept in her fancy parlor. I made a nest for it in her best china, and guess what happened."

"No!" I gasped, already guessing.

"Mmmhmm." She nodded. "I dropped it and destroyed a whole tea set."

"I . . . I'm just like you?"

"Just like me," my grandma confirmed, putting a flour-coated arm around my shoulders. "A Jenkins woman through and through."

"No," I said thoughtfully. "Also a Lee."

The next day I was at my Nai Nai and Ye Ye's house, and I helped my Nai Nai make dumplings while my Ye Ye worked in his woodshop.

My Nai Nai rolled the dough and put the dumpling balls inside, and it was my job to pinch them shut at the top. Which gave me time to think, and to watch my Nai Nai's hands move fast and quick, a blur of lots of colors too—yellow and white and pink and bits of brown and red.

"Nai Nai," I said. "Do you mind that I don't look like you?"

"Ay yah!" She stopped rolling and turned to me, putting one of her hands on mine. "You are my beautiful granddaughter. What would I mind?"

"But I'm . . ." I tried again. "Different from you."

"Not so different," she tutted, patting my hand. "You know, your dad told me about your mom's shoes."

"You mean the heels and the dirt and the worms?" I asked, feeling my face get a little red.

"Yes." She nodded. "When I was little, I was very curious, just like you. I want to test everything. So, one day, I took all our shoes. I went to the tallest window, and—wah!"

"You threw them?!" I gasped.

"Yes!" She laughed. "To see if they would fly."

"Did they?" I asked, feeling my eyes get wide at the idea of my Nai Nai doing something like that.

"No." She smiled again, looking maybe a little embarrassed. "They fell in the mud."

"Oh no!" I exclaimed.

"Yes," she said.

I giggled. "I can't believe it. I'm just like you!"

"A true Lee," she said, giving me a kiss on the head.

"No," I corrected her, softly. "And a Jenkins."

On Monday, Ms. Bloom stood in front of the class and said, "Well, everyone. Did you get a chance to think about your colors this weekend?"

And I knew for once I wasn't exaggerating or making anything up when I sighed and said, "Yes," slumping back in my chair. "It was *exhausting*."

**A week later, we had our end-of-the-year** party. My mom and dad came, and we took pictures, and ate cookies, and all the parents admired our drawings, and Colleen's mom said I'd drawn my expression "just right," which was a nice thing to hear. I could see the space between my mom's eyes frown a little, though, when she saw my picture. But then she smiled, and said she loved it.

When all the celebrations were done, and she was tucking me into bed that night, my mom said,

"We'll have to keep in touch with Ms. Bloom." She sat on the edge of my bed and smoothed the hair away from my face. "What a sharp woman. I like her a lot."

"Me too," I replied.

"Your classroom was so pretty," she went on. "And I spotted your drawing the second we walked in. Do you want to put it up somewhere? How about on your wall, or on the fridge?"

"Maybe later." I shrugged. I didn't know if I really wanted to see it every day.

"It's a lovely picture, sweetie," she said. Then she paused. "I love the way you drew Horatio's hat, you got the shape just right. And the red is so bright and cheery. Only . . . everyone's so far apart."

"Yes." I sighed. "I didn't mean for that to happen." I was going to say something else, but then I saw that frowning, worried look again.

So I kept quiet.

And later, after she'd given me a hug and said

good night, I lay in bed, thinking about what I hadn't said to my mom.

Because I really didn't mean for my family to be so far apart in my picture.

But I think it's maybe just how they want to be.

# STRUGGLES

**School is over now, and Ms. Bloom promised** to visit us in third grade, which made me feel better about saying goodbye. Also, Colleen and I are going to be in the same class next year (Alien-Face too), which I'm excited about.

Since school ended, I've been doing a lot of things. I went on vacation with my mom and dad, and we visited the beach every day. We had a great time, and even though I brought my notebook to write in, I didn't because I was so busy making sand castles and eating ice cream. But then, when we were getting ready to come home, even though I told my mom I'd double-check that I'd packed everything, I didn't because I was imagining that the squeaky wheels on my suitcase were mice with super-human (or mouse) strength. So I *left my notebook* in our hotel room, and it was TERRIBLE because what if someone else found it and pretended it was theirs and published it and became a bestselling author with MY stories?!

Luckily, this didn't happen. And the hotel mailed it back to me, which was very nice of them. But it only just arrived, which means that I'm *really* behind with my writing.

After I got back from vacation, I started camp. Camp is A LOT of fun. Colleen's there too, and we get to swim in the community pool and play games in a big field. We also do arts and crafts, and last week I learned how to make a picture frame and a friendship bracelet, which are two excellent skills to have.

But not even camp or getting my notebook back could make this week any better.

On Tuesday, I helped my mom pack her bag for

the hospital, which was (just a little, only slightly) fun. I wanted my mom to pack her high heels because they're great, and you can barely see where they got scratched in the dirt. Plus, if you're going to insist on having a new baby, you might as well be fancy about it.

My mom didn't agree with this, but she promised that she'd wear heels to The Blob's one-month party. (When a baby is one month old, you have a big banquet in Chinatown to celebrate. I love banquets. Waiters bring out new plates of delicious food ALL THE TIME, and you eat at tables that have a big circle in the middle that spins. Spinning it really fast and trying to spear food with your chopsticks while it goes is an EXCELLENT game, though sometimes it makes a mess on your great-aunt's party dress).

While we packed, we talked about what was going to happen later that weekend—a *sleepover* at Colleen's house.

When Colleen invited me for a sleepover, it was

hard to know what to say. She and I have been talk-ing about me sleeping over for a loooong time, because even though sleepovers at my house are fun, Colleen's parents have a machine that makes WAFFLES, and her mom said that if I stay over, she'll make us some for breakfast. Also, Colleen has LOTS of board games, and we planned to stay up all night and play them. This has always sounded fun, and I really, really wanted to go.

But then I remembered the last time I tried to stay over, and how scared I was, and worse, how hard it was to explain to Colleen that I was scared of being in the dark. And even though Colleen said she was sorry for calling me a baby that day on the bus, I still think about it sometimes. And I want her to know that I'm not a baby—I'm her best friend.

That's why, when Colleen sleeps over at my house, I do things like hide my nightlight and ask my mom to leave the hall light on and the door open a little, and to say it's for Colleen so she'll know where the bathroom is.

So I said yes to Colleen and the sleepover. And then I thought about asking my mom if she could tell Colleen's parents that I couldn't go after all (I invented an EXCELLENT story to use as an excuse, involving the chicken pox and a hot-air balloon with a bank robber inside). But when I got home that day, Colleen's mom had already called my mom to schedule everything, and my mom told me how proud she was of me for saying yes (which was nice). And she gave me a hug and told me that she and my dad would always be there to come and get me if I needed them (which was nicer).

So, while my mom packed for the hospital, I started to plan what I would pack for Colleen's. My dad had to work late that night, so my mom and I had a special evening all to ourselves. After we packed her suitcase, we ate pizza and played checkers (though we got bored and ended up making a game to see how many checker pieces we could balance on my mom's stomach. The answer is A LOT.).

The next morning, my dad walked me to the camp bus stop and he and I sang all our favorite songs on the way, and then Colleen and I were paired together for a relay race. It was a fun day, even if I was still nervous about the sleepover later in the week, and wondering if I could bring my unicorn poster with me, because at least that would mean I wouldn't have to worry about Colleen's closet.

But I was trying to forget about these worries, and mostly I was doing a very good job and having an excellent time. Until, just as Colleen and I were getting in line for the bus to go home, and making up a story about how we were brave explorers on a jungle safari who could talk to lions, one of the counselors came over and said, "Cilla, there's someone here for you."

I looked around. There, by the door, was my Grandma Jenkins. And even though she was trying to smile, she had a worried look on her face.

Suddenly, I didn't feel brave like an explorer anymore.

My Grandma Jenkins came over and gave me a big hug, and said, "Everything's fine, Cilla. We're going to go see your mom and dad in the hospital, and I'll explain everything in the car."

My mom hadn't had The Blob (which at first I was relieved to hear, because I really don't want it to come yet, even if it would be good timing, because my birthday isn't for another two weeks). But she was on something called "bed rest," which meant that she needed to lie down all the time. And she had to stay at the hospital so the doctors and nurses could check on her until the baby was born.

It took me a minute to understand what my grandma was saying, because I was busy feeling angry at The Blob.

But then what she said finally sank in.

"Wait," I said as I realized what she meant, and my voice was the small one that comes out sometimes that I don't like. "Mom's not coming home?"

"Not until your sister is born," my grandma said, in a voice that was different from her normal one too, like she was trying to be very soft and calm. "It shouldn't be too long now. And while she's gone, we'll all be there to look after you."

"Will Dad come home?" I asked, my voice still small. My grandma didn't seem to mind, even though she hates mumbling and likes to say things like "Speak up, dear" or "Enunciate, please" whenever you're too quiet.

"Your father's going to spend most of his time at the hospital so he can keep your mother company," she answered. "He's already packed a bag with your things, and you're going to spend tonight with your grandfather and me, and then tomorrow night with your other grandparents. He's told me all about your sleepover plans too, for the night after. And you'll get to visit your mother every afternoon in the hospital."

I didn't know what to say. So instead I just looked out the window.

"Cilla," my grandma said, "are you all right? Do you want to talk about it?"

"No," I said. And I didn't.

"It's going to be fine," she said.

But I didn't say anything back.

I didn't like the hospital. It was big and gray with lots of small windows, and inside everything was white and all the people wore funny outfits. It didn't seem like a place that my mom would like, and I held my grandma's hand very tight, especially when a man came by with a bed that was on *wheels*. Because even though this was a fun idea in theory (and I bet racing down a hill on a bed with wheels would be GREAT), I didn't like the idea of my mom being in one of those beds instead of being home with me. So I hid my face in my grandma's sweater until we were past him.

When we got to my mom's hallway, I saw my dad and Grandpa Jenkins talking by a doorway. And I was maybe a little bit rude, because I didn't say hi to Grandpa Jenkins right away. I was too busy running to my dad and getting picked up in a big hug. Grandpa Jenkins seemed okay with this, though.

My mom's room wasn't as bad as I thought it'd be, and even though her bed had wheels, it also had a button that could make the end where her head was higher or lower, which was fun.

Grandpa Jenkins sat in one corner flipping through TV channels (there was a TV *hanging from the ceiling*, which was very impressive) and Grandma Jenkins sat in the other corner reorganizing my mom's suitcase. ("It's okay," my mom whispered to my dad. "If she doesn't have a project she'll drive me up the wall." I wondered how this would work, especially because my mom is VERY heavy because of The Blob right now, so probably she'd fall down from the wall. But it didn't seem like the time to ask.)

My dad sat next to the bed and helped me up, and my mom and I cuddled.

So, I decided to feel better, especially because when I lay next to her, I didn't have to look at the needles that were taped into her arm. She said they were good because they were giving her medicine, but I didn't like them AT ALL.

"Do you still want to stay at Colleen's?" my dad asked. "You don't have to if you don't want to—all your grandparents would love to have you."

"Colleen's is fine," I said quietly. "But I wish I could be home with you."

"The baby will be here before you know it," my mom said, trying to make me smile. "Maybe even tomorrow. Then we'll all be together!"

"Okay," I whispered.

"I know it's hard, sweetheart," my mom said. "You're being so brave." This was nice to hear. But I didn't think I believed it.

That night, Grandma and Grandpa Jenkins took me to their house, and my Grandma Jenkins cooked steak and spinach and mashed potatoes, and my Grandpa Jenkins went out to buy an ice cream cake as a special treat. I got to have a bubble bath, and my Grandma Jenkins read me stories for a whole *hour*, and then she plugged in my dinosaur night-light, which my dad had packed for me (because he's the best). It made green and blue patterns on the wall, just like it does in my room. But it wasn't home.

The next day, my Ye Ye picked me up from camp, and we drove to the hospital to see my mom. Nai Nai was there (with almond cookies!), and she and Ye Ye and my dad sat by the window and talked in Chinese, while my mom and I cuddled, and I told her all about camp that day.

That night, I went home to my Nai Nai and Ye Ye's house. Nai Nai cooked sausage in rice, and Ye Ye bought white buns and dried pork for breakfast the next day (another one of my favorite things).

I sang songs with my Nai Nai and I drew her a

picture that made her say "Wah!" so I knew I'd
done a great job. Then I helped her pull out the
fold-up couch (which is a couch that turns into a
bed, which is AMAZING, plus when the bed's
unfolded is the only time you're allowed to make
a fort out of couch pillows, since no one needs
them for sitting). Ye Ye read to me, and Nai Nai

sat by my bed and sang me my favorite Chinese lullaby. And my nightlight lit the living room, and I could hear Nai Nai and Ye Ye whispering in Chinese in the next room as I closed my eyes, and that's a very nice sound to fall asleep to. But it wasn't home, either.

The next morning, I helped Nai Nai pack a smaller bag with my pajamas, my toothbrush, and a change of clothes. Nai Nai reached over to my dinosaur nightlight, and was about to put it in the bag, when I said, "No. I'll leave it here."

"Are you sure?" she asked.

I was.

I held my Nai Nai's hand extra tight when she dropped me off at camp that morning, and I gave her a big hug goodbye. And that afternoon, I went home with Colleen for my first-ever sleepover.

I've spent lots of time at Colleen's house before. But this was the first time I'd unpacked my toothbrush in her bathroom, or picked a towel from her closet (Colleen guessed rightly that I'd choose the towel with a rainbow-colored WHALE, which was very exciting).

Dinner was a lot of fun, and Colleen's dad told us jokes, and Colleen and I told everyone all about the water balloon toss (it was even better than we'd hoped. We got to throw water balloons *at* Alien-Face McGee, and since it was part of a game, we didn't even get in trouble.).

We played board games after dinner (though apparently, our plan to play board games all night long was Not Going to Happen, according to Colleen's mom). And when it was my turn to shower, Colleen let me play with the plastic cap she sometimes wears, and I pretended it was an astronaut's helmet.

But there was a nervous feeling in my stomach the whole time, because this wasn't my house, and even though I've been to Colleen's before, I still sometimes forget where things are and get lost.

Finally, the moment I'd been dreading came. Colleen's mom told us that it was time for lights-out, and even though I'd talked with my mom and dad that night on the phone to say "hello" and "I miss you," what if I got scared and wanted to go home? Colleen would think I was a baby, and then even if I did want to go, who would come and get me? And why did everything have to be so different?

Colleen's mom gave us both hugs (which was very nice of her) and said good night. I closed my eyes and scrunched up my face as she flicked off the light.

"Are you okay, Cilla?" Colleen asked.

"Yes," I said, trying to be brave. I took a deep breath, and opened my eyes, preparing myself for the dark . . .

. . . but I saw STARS instead, bright and white, *glowing in the dark from Colleen's ceiling.*

"Wow," I gasped.

"Do you like them?" Colleen said, and it was funny, because her voice sounded a little nervous.

"I LOVE them," I said.

"I thought . . ." Colleen hesitated. "I thought you might think they were silly. Or that they might bother you and keep you from falling asleep. The thing is, sometimes . . . I get a little scared of the dark."

I turned to look at her, my eyes big.

"I'm getting better," she said quickly. "I'm only scared sometimes, I swear. I don't want you to think I'm a baby, it's just that—"

"Colleen," I said. "*I'm* scared of the dark."

Her eyes were big now too. "But when I slept over—"

"I hid my nightlight," I confessed. "In my sock drawer."

Colleen thought this over for a minute. Then she giggled. And I giggled, too.

"What kind of nightlight?" she asked.

"A dinosaur," I answered. "He's blue with green polka dots. I named him Herman."

"I can't wait to meet him," she said, lying back on her pillows. Then, "Also," she said after another minute, "the stars are really fun for making up stories if you can't sleep. Sometimes I look up at them and imagine I'm in outer space."

We lay there for a little while. I turned to Colleen again, and I could just see her outline under the soft glow of the ceiling.

"I'm glad you're my friend, Colleen," I said, in a quiet voice.

"I'm glad you're my friend too, Cilla," she said back.

A few minutes later, I could tell she was asleep. (Colleen snores, which makes me giggle. But I giggled quietly, so I wouldn't wake her up. I'm a good best friend that way.)

I felt a lot better. But I still missed home. And I was still worried about my mom. And this still wasn't my house, and what if I had to go to the bathroom and couldn't remember which room was Colleen's, and then had to wander through the hallways for the rest of eternity?! (Or at least the rest of the night.)

So I made up a story to tell myself. It was about a baby brontosaurus who's afraid of heights, and whose best friend is a bird. His best friend is kidnapped by pterodactyls, and the brontosaurus has to conquer his fears, and there's a chase scene, and he saves his friend, and he finds out he's not really a brontosaurus after all—he's a baby dragon and has wings. And he and his best friend fly off together, underneath the stars, and they're very happy. And there's a car chase, and explosions, and aliens, and . . .

. . . and then I fell asleep . . .

. . . and woke up to the sound of the telephone ringing.

# NEW THINGS

Colleen was just starting to wake up when I came running back into her room, so I helped her wake up some more by jumping onto her bed and bouncing.

"My dad just called," I said, in a low voice, as if it were a secret. "My mom's having the baby." And I was surprised, because even though I had a nervous feeling in my stomach, I was smiling too, and Colleen gave me a big hug and started bouncing on the bed with me. And then I told her how I'd heard the phone ring and snuck downstairs, and how her mom had hung up the phone and given me a big hug and told me that my mom was in labor, which means the baby is about to come (even though it's not Labor Day, which in this case I was VERY HAPPY about).

We ate breakfast in our pajamas (I got to help turn the handle of the waffle machine), and Colleen's dad made us hot chocolate with whipped cream on top, because he said it was a special occasion. I was a little quiet, but Colleen understood.

After breakfast, Colleen convinced her brother Matt to play at being a baby, and she taught me how to hold him. This was a little hard, because Matt is three and kept getting bored and wiggling and sometimes trying to do a backflip. But playing babies was actually really fun, and Colleen's mom sat on the couch reading a book, and every once in a while saying things like "Not upside down!" and "Did you just put a diaper on your brother's head?" (The answer to that question was yes, because Matt still wears diapers, and I wanted to see how they worked, and Colleen thought it would be funny if we practiced by making a hat. Matt liked this too, and didn't take his hat off for the rest of the morning, and Colleen's mom sighed and sounded just like my mom, which was funny.) Then Colleen's other brother, Josh, who's six, wanted a turn at being the baby, plus the chance to wear a special hat. And then Matt wanted to hold a baby, so we pretended he could hold me, even though I could probably squish him (which I guess really and truly makes me a big kid).

I'd never spent much time playing with Colleen's brothers (usually we try to hide from them so they won't interrupt our games), and I was surprised by how much I liked it. I even promised Matt that he could hold a real live baby when my sister came home from the hospital. And when Colleen's brothers ran off to play a different game (they're something her mom calls "high energy"), Colleen sat next to me and said, "I didn't mean to scare you about being a Big Sister and all the Responsibilities. It can be fun. I think you'll be really good at it."

I couldn't think of anything to say, so I just put

my head on her shoulder, which seemed like enough. And then, all of a sudden, the phone rang again, and Colleen's mom was shouting, "Cilla, it's for you!"

**Later that morning, my dad came to get me,** just like he'd said he would on the phone. He gave me a big hug and spun me around, and then he carried me to the car, which I let him do even if I am officially a big kid.

We drove to the hospital, which I'm getting to know very well now, and I waved at the window where (I think) my mom's room was. We went inside, and I didn't hide my face when the beds with wheels came by.

And when we turned down the hallway to my mom's room, I held my dad's hand a bit tighter, because I saw something I'd never seen before—my Grandma and Grandpa Jenkins *and* my Nai Nai and Ye Ye, all sitting on chairs in the hallway. My

Nai Nai and Ye Ye were sitting on one side, talking in Chinese, and my Grandma and Grandpa Jenkins were on the other side, doing a crossword puzzle.

But I didn't have (too) much time to stop and feel strange about seeing them all there together, because I was too busy running toward them, yelling, "What does she look like? Does she have hair? How much? Can she talk? Is she big? Is she nice?"

"We don't know," my Ye Ye said, laughing and giving me a hug.

"You haven't met her yet?" I asked, confused.

"Why no, Cilla dear," my Grandma Jenkins said, putting her arm around me. "You're her big sister. Which means you get to meet her first."

"Oh," I said. Suddenly, I felt shy.

"Come on." My dad put his arm around me. "Your mom's really excited to see you."

So we walked into the room. My mom was in bed and looked tired but happy, and she gave me a big hug. And then she kept her arm around me while my dad went over to what I'd thought was a table in the corner, but was really a little basket attached to a table, and he took out what looked like a small, rolled-up blanket. But it was my new little sister.

I sat in one of the hospital chairs, scooched all the way back, with my legs dangling in the air, and my dad put a blanket on my lap. And then he brought the baby over, and I held her, just like Colleen had taught me.

She was much, much smaller than I'd thought she'd be, and her face was all wrinkled and scrunched, which was a bit disappointing. In fact, she WAS like a Blob. She also had more hair than the picture of her in my mom's stomach had let on, which wasn't really that fair. But she looked a lot friendlier than she had in that picture too. And she made small sighing noises, and she smelled like powder and clean things.

So even though when my parents asked what I

thought I shrugged and said, "She's okay," I didn't give her back right away. I rocked her very gently, like Colleen's mom had shown me, and I said, "Hello, Blob." And my dad opened his mouth like he was going to say something, but I could see my mom shake her head and give him a Parent Look from across the room, and then he didn't say anything at all. So it can't have been that important.

Then, when I was ready, my dad called my grandparents in, and they took turns meeting my new little sister.

My mom and dad were very tired, and my grandparents were busy meeting The Blob and rearranging the flowers on my mom's window ledge. (This was just Grandma Jenkins, actually. Also, I didn't bring flowers because I didn't know you were supposed to, but my mom says that the story I wrote for her was better than flowers, so that was good. It was about a walrus, in the end.)

One of the nurses brought me a Popsicle, which was very nice of her. And it meant I could just sit quietly on the edge of my mom's bed, eating my Popsicle and holding her hand. She was busy talking to my Grandpa Jenkins and every once in a while saying things like, "Mom, give it a rest," when my Grandma Jenkins tried to fluff her pillow or organize her bedside table. My dad and Nai Nai spoke quietly in the corner in Chinese, my Nai Nai rocking The Blob, and my Ye Ye came over to sit by me.

"How was the sleepover?" he asked.

"It was fun," I said softly.

"What did you do?"

"We played games," I said. "Oh, and we made *waffles*," and then I didn't feel so quiet anymore, and I told him all about Colleen's house, and the stars, and the dinosaur story (which he liked). I also told him about how Colleen's mom made vegetable stew, which was delicious, and which reminded me of tzuck sang, which is around when my stomach began to make a rumbling sound, because it had been a while since I'd eaten, and Popsicles aren't very filling (even if they are delicious).

"You know," Ye Ye said, looking over at my dad, "Chinatown isn't very far away. We could get lunch there and celebrate."

"Yes!" I said, excited. "And we could get tzuck sang, and steamed tofu, and salt and pepper pork, and—"

I stopped suddenly. Because I'd forgotten that it wasn't just me and my mom and dad and Nai Nai and Ye Ye. My Grandma and Grandpa Jenkins were there too. And they wouldn't come to Chinatown, and would they feel left out? The room suddenly felt small, with all those people in it, and kind of quiet, too.

"Would you join us?" Ye Ye turned to them, smiling but with a funny sound to his voice that I realized was *his* Best Behavior. "We were just talking about taking Cilla to lunch, and Chinatown is very close. Though"—he looked uncertainly at my Grandma and Grandpa Jenkins—"we could go somewhere else too."

And then all the adults (except for Nai Nai, who was busy kissing The Blob on the cheek) started talking at once.

"Oh, we wouldn't want to intrude." (Grandpa Jenkins)

"We would love to have you." (Ye Ye)

"Kind offer, though." (Dad)

"...needs our help settling in after all the excitement. Why, the bed's already come unmade again, and I haven't seen the nurse for ages..." (Grandma Jenkins)

"You know what?" Mom spoke the loudest of them all. "You should ALL go."

"But—" my dad started.

"I'm exhausted, Nathan. I'm just going to sleep," my mom interrupted him. "You should go and be with *everyone*." And just then my Grandma Jenkins started refolding the blankets at the end of my mom's bed, and my mom gave my Dad a look that made him say "Okay" very fast.

Which is how I ended up in Chinatown with my dad, my Grandma and Grandpa Jenkins, AND my Nai Nai and Ye Ye.

## SURPRISES

**I didn't know how to feel about this.**

I leaned against my dad's arm and rested my head on his shoulder, while Ye Ye explained the menu to Grandma and Grandpa Jenkins. I was glad that no one was talking to me. Because even though I was with some of the people I love most and know best in the whole world, things didn't feel right. What if Ye Ye slurped his soup, or Grandma Jenkins asked for a fork, or Grandpa Jenkins thought the food was gross? What were we all going to talk about, and what if *I* was different around each of them? What if Nai Nai and Ye Ye didn't like the jokes I told around Grandma and Grandpa Jenkins, or Grandma and Grandpa Jenkins didn't like the games I played with Nai Nai and Ye Ye, like making chopstick holders, or being silly with the spinning circle in the middle of the table?

And even though I'd spent all that time wishing my grandparents could be together, I suddenly wished I could just be with my mom and dad, but not in the hospital, at *home* . . .

When suddenly, I heard my Grandma Jenkins say something in a loud, happy voice—something that wasn't English, but wasn't Chinese, either.

"*Escargot!* What a treat."

I looked up. She and my Ye Ye were smiling about something.

"What's that?" I asked, suspiciously. "Are you sure it's something you can get in Chinatown, Grandma?"

"*Escargot,*" my grandma said excitedly, "is one of my favorite foods, and it's French for snails. Now I know it sounds odd," she said quickly, "but it's really quite delicious."

"Oh," my dad said, patting my back and smiling, "Cilla's had snails before."

"Really?" Grandma Jenkins said. "I'm impressed, Cilla. That's a very sophisticated dish. I'm excited to try the Chinese version."

"Oh" was all I could say.

"Well, if you like snails, you should try . . . ," my Nai Nai cut in. And then she and my grandma started talking about the menu, and they both seemed much more like they normally do, even if they were also a little too polite. And my Grandma Jenkins did an EXCELLENT job pretending to be interested when my Nai Nai suggested we get beef intestines soup. (We didn't order that one in the end, which I think was a good choice.) While they talked, my dad leaned over to my Grandpa Jenkins and whispered, "Don't worry, we'll get pork fried rice too," and Grandpa looked so relieved that I giggled.

Ye Ye ordered for us all in Chinese, and it turns out that Grandpa Jenkins can use chopsticks, which was very impressive. And even though Grandma Jenkins doesn't know how to use them, she loved the chopstick holders we made and asked me to teach her how to fold one. When the food came, my Nai Nai piled my plate high with white rice and tzuck sang like she always does. And then she stopped with her chopsticks halfway out to another dish, and turned to me, with her eyebrow raised and a question on her face.

I smiled and said, "Yes, please," and Nai Nai gave me a big smile back. And soon we were all happily eating our lunch of rice, tofu, salt and pepper pork, beef with bitter melon, tzuck sang, and snails.

Grandpa Jenkins ate mostly fried rice, though he did try the tzuck sang and liked it. (He wouldn't try the snails, but I told him not to worry—tastes change, after all. His just weren't sophisticated enough yet.) And even though Grandma Jenkins raised her eyebrows when Ye Ye picked up his soup bowl and slurped, she didn't say anything, and when my Grandpa Jenkins put soy sauce all over his fried rice, Nai Nai acted like she hadn't seen him do it.

After lunch, we went back to the hospital to see my mom. She and The Blob have to stay there for a few more days, which is sad. But my dad was coming home with me, which was EXCELLENT news.

My grandparents started saying goodbye, and my dad said I could hold The Blob again, so I went back to the chair, with the blanket on my lap, and took another look at my little sister. She stared back up at me with tiny eyes and round cheeks that were soft and smooth when I touched them with my finger.

And I was surprised, because she really didn't seem all that bad.

But as I looked up from The Blob's scrunched-up face, out the open door of my mom's hospital room, I saw something that surprised me even more.

I saw my Nai Nai and my Grandma Jenkins standing in the hallway, and I saw my Nai Nai *whisper* something to my Grandma Jenkins. Grandma Jenkins nodded and whispered something back.

Then they walked away from the door and down the hall, their heads close together.

I watched them go. And even though this is what I've wanted all along, I didn't feel happy.

I felt *sad*.

I've always wanted my family to be a family, a real one that spends time together and talks and whispers and goes to lunch.

But no matter how much I've wanted this, or how many stories I've told to each of my grandparents about how great the others are, the two sides of my family have always stayed far apart. So I thought that was just how they were meant to be.

But it turns out now that isn't true. It turns out that my family *can* be together. I just wasn't enough, on my own, to make this happen. I'm their granddaughter, and a future author extraordinaire, and a Lee-Jenkins.

But it took The Blob to make my family want to be a family.

So I watched my grandmas go, and there was

something tight and sad inside my throat. But I had another surprise, because just then, The Blob made a soft, sighing sound, and I looked down.

And even though I was still sad, and worried about having to share my family and my house and my toys, I looked at The Blob and realized that maybe my little sister will never have to draw a family picture like the one I drew. Maybe the people in her portrait will stay together on the page.

And this made me want to hold my sister a little tighter, and a little longer. Which seemed to be okay with her, because she smiled, and then right before my eyes, and in my arms, fell asleep. Which was nice. (She snores too, apparently, which also made me giggle, but quietly, so I wouldn't wake her up. I'm a good Big Sister that way.)

**That night, I said goodbye to my mom and** The Blob, and got in the car with my dad, to finally—after *three whole days*—go home. And even though I was still feeling confused and a little sad, as the car turned on and started to make rumbling noises, I realized that I was tired, too. So I closed my eyes, and I could smell the good smells coming from the bag of leftovers, which Nai Nai had insisted we take home. And as I fell asleep, I told myself another story. This time not a made-up story, but a real-life one—about going home, about my dad tucking me into bed, and about the delicious lunch I would eat the next day, of tzuck sang and escargot.

# TRADITIONS

**We have a lot of traditions in my family, and** several have changed since The Blob came home. For example, my dad and I used to cook breakfast for my mom on Sundays. Then we'd all eat breakfast in their bed, and then my dad would take me to the park to play. My mom and I would go grocery shopping on the weekends too, and our grocery store is AMAZING because kids get a free cookie at the bakery from a woman named Donna, and I'd get to push the shopping cart before it got too heavy.

But now that The Blob's here, my dad was too tired on Sunday to go to the park or to cook, and so we just had cereal, but my mom didn't eat with us because The Blob started crying. And my dad went to the grocery store on his way home from work, because my mom was too tired to go (which is a big theme in our house lately). So I didn't get to go with him, or get a cookie, or say hello to Donna.

There are also new traditions about sleep and noise (there's a lot less sleep and I have to make a lot less noise, which doesn't seem fair since The Blob makes SO MUCH of it). There's also the tradition of changing diapers, which is interesting and happens on a special table but makes some TERRIBLE smells. I'm hoping that one doesn't last long.

But there are some nice new traditions too. For example, every morning I get to help dress The Blob (and she looks AMAZING. My general rule is that she should be wearing as many colors and patterns as possible.). And, BEST of all, my mom and dad have told me that because I'm being so great about helping, they're going to *change* the no-sugary-breakfast-cereal rule. The next time they go to the grocery store, they're going to buy me a box of Choco-Rex that's ALL for me, and I can eat it WHENEVER I WANT. This has been maybe the most exciting part about being a Big Sister so far.

There are some traditions, though, that I don't think will ever change. They're called family traditions, and all my grandparents are REALLY strict about them. For example, once a year I get a red envelope with a whole ten dollars inside from my Nai Nai and Ye Ye. This is fun because I love presents, and because it involves going to my Ye Ye's favorite restaurant, which has a giant dragon statue in the lobby. On the wall. With glowing green eyes. And you can't find much that's better for the imagination than that. Also, there are fireworks. On the red envelope day, which is called Chinese New Year, the fireworks are tied to string, and men light them in the streets, and my mom says, "Keep your distance, Cilla," and the fireworks go "Pop pop pop!" and flash in little puffs of smoke.

These kinds of fireworks are very different than

the fireworks we get to see during another family tradition, which is the Fourth of July. It's our family tradition to go to my Grandma and Grandpa Jenkins's house on the Fourth of July. We eat hamburgers and yellow cake decorated with whipped cream, strawberries, and blueberries in the shape of a flag. This is a great family tradition, because it's delicious.

Sometimes, there are traditions on both sides of my family on the very same day, like Thanksgiving. In the afternoon, we go to my Nai Nai and Ye Ye's, who have us over, along with all their friends from Chinatown. We sit everywhere—at the table, in the living room, on the floor, on the couch—and eat turkey and rice and spareribs and bok choy. All the food is piled on one big table and none of the plates match.

After afternoon Thanksgiving with my Nai Nai and Ye Ye, we get in the car and go to my Grandma and Grandpa Jenkins's house, where my mom reminds us to "act hungry." There, we sit at the dining room table (which is somehow more special than the kitchen one, though I don't quite understand why), and we eat off fancy plates with gold at their edges. By the end of the day, I am VERY full of turkey, mashed potatoes, and pumpkin pie, not to mention the soy sauce chicken, sticky rice stuffing, and roasted duck.

I like family traditions. They're fun, plus you get to dress up in your prettiest grown-up clothes. And eat A TON.

So when my Grandpa Jenkins told me about a new tradition this past weekend that I'd never heard about, I was excited to try it. We were staying with Grandma and Grandpa Jenkins so my grandma could help with the baby.

That day, I was upstairs playing with the dollhouse that my grandparents keep for me. Dollhouses are great for making up stories, and I was in the middle of an epic drama that had Suspense and five main characters, three love interests, ten children, two imaginary dogs, and my teddy bear as an all-powerful dragon.

"Cilla." Grandpa Jenkins interrupted my story. "I was wondering if you'd like to come on a special walk with me."

"A walk?" I didn't even look up, that's how exciting my doll story was. "I don't know, I'm kind of busy right now. . . ."

"Oh, it's not just an everyday kind of walk," he said. "This walk is part of a very old, long-standing town tradition."

I looked up. "A tradition?" He had my attention now.

"Yes, a tradition," he said, sitting down on the edge of the playroom couch.

"You see, your grandma and I live in a very old town. And there's a custom that dates all the way back, hundreds of years ago, to the first people who lived here. Every Sunday afternoon, without fail, the townspeople dress in their finest clothes and go for a walk in the local park, the one right by the old bridge."

I considered this for a moment.

"Why haven't we done it before?"

"Well," my grandpa said, scratching his head, "because you're usually not here on Sundays. And, most of all, because this tradition is very old and special. You have to do it right. So I didn't want to suggest it if you didn't have your Sunday best to wear. That wouldn't have been fair to you. But, as luck would have it, your grandma told me that you brought a very special dress here this weekend."

"Yes!" I exclaimed, suddenly excited. "My cheongsam! I just got it as an early birthday present, and it's for special occasions."

"Golly!" Grandpa Jenkins exclaimed. "What luck!"

**And so my Grandpa Jenkins and I left the** house a half hour later, my grandpa looking fancy in a white suit, gold vest, red bow tie, and white handkerchief with yellow and red stripes in his pocket. On his head he wore what he calls his "finest fedora," and he carried a brown cane with a silver horse head on top.

I had on my brand-new red cheongsam. It's long
and narrow at the bottom, with buttons made of
cloth that loop at your neck. Mine has gold patterns all over, and it's the most beautiful thing I
own. I've wanted a cheongsam for the looooongest
time, and my Nai Nai and Ye Ye decided that nine

was grown-up enough to finally get one. And even though my birthday isn't for another four-and-a-half days, they gave it to me early because they were too excited to wait, plus I've been so good about helping with The Blob.

In a cheongsam, it's easy to feel like a princess (no glitter glue required this time), and it just so happened that my mom had brought my fancy gold slippers. ("I thought your grandma might like to see the whole outfit," she said, "and just threw them in at the last minute." "Golly," I'd replied. "What luck!")

Grandpa Jenkins and I set off, dried leaves swirling at our feet.

"To the bridge!" he said, pointing ahead with his cane. I took his arm and felt very grown-up.

"So, Cilla," he said as we strolled (which is a fancy word for "walking"), "what have you been up to this past week? Oh, good morning." He tipped his hat to some people on the street who were looking at us.

"*They're* not dressed up," I observed.

"Well, we're not at the park yet."

"Ah." I nodded, skipping along beside him.

"Well," I began, "this week's been very good." I told him about the last week of camp, and about getting a letter that told me my third-grade teacher is called Mr. Flight, which is exciting because I wonder if he's a pilot, or has wings.

"Good morning," a couple walking by said, smiling at us.

"Good morning!" I waved back happily, though I turned to my grandpa and whispered in a very soft voice, so they wouldn't feel bad, "They're not dressed up either. And they've just left the park."

"Young people these days," he said, shaking his head. "They have no respect for traditions."

"Terrible." I shook my head too and made a *tsk*-ing noise like him. Then I waved at another couple who had just noticed us in our Sunday best and were probably feeling bad because they weren't dressed up either.

"I've been spending a lot of time at home, and at Colleen's house, because Mom and Dad are too tired to do things like go to the park or the zoo," I went on. "But it's okay."

"Well," Grandpa Jenkins said, "your mom tells me you're being just wonderful with the baby."

"I guess." I shrugged. "I like it more than I thought I would," I admitted. "But taking care of a little sister seems like a lot of work and responsibilities."

"Well." Grandpa Jenkins thought for a minute. "It's true that there are a lot of responsibilities attached. But it can be fun, too. And you also have a pretty big influence, you know, as a big sister."

"Really?" I asked, not quite believing him.

"It's true," he said. "Why, the things you teach her, and the stories you tell her, will really matter. You know, my older sister, your great-aunt Annette, had me convinced that I wasn't really her brother. She told me that I'd been left on the doorstep by fairies or elves, and I believed her until I was five or six. Not that you should do that," he added quickly. "She got in trouble when our parents found out."

"Huh . . ." I said. Great-aunt Annette is pretty great (which makes sense, I guess, because it's in her name). She does magic tricks at the dinner table, which makes my grandma make *tsk*ing noises, but she does them anyway, which is very brave. I didn't know that she told stories too (*excellent* ones, for that matter). And I'd forgotten that Great-aunt Annette is my grandpa's sister, and I'd *definitely* forgotten that my Grandpa Jenkins is a *little brother*.

"Oh, good morning." My grandpa nodded to a group of women smiling in our direction.

"Don't you two look lovely!" one of the women exclaimed.

"Thank you," I replied. "It's a tradition."

"Have a nice morning, ladies," my grandpa said, touching his hat, which is a fancy way of saying hello and goodbye, and we kept walking.

"Grandpa, those women weren't even 'young people,' and they weren't dressed up either!" I put my hands on my hips. "Something has to be done!"

"Well, we'll just have to lead by example, Cilla, my dear," my grandpa said, glancing at his watch. His horse-head cane made *click-click-click*ing sounds as it hit the wooden boards of the old bridge.

"Maybe I will like the baby someday," I said,

stopping with him at the center of the bridge to look out over the small river that runs through his town. "I like it more now, *especially* because I don't have to share my birthday."

"Yes," my grandpa said, looking out over the water. "Only a few days to go—are you excited?"

I nodded. "Mom says I'll get to celebrate with you and Grandma Jenkins the night before, which I'm happy about. I asked for chocolate cake."

"Mmmmmm," my Grandpa Jenkins said.

"Yes," I agreed. "Then I'll celebrate with Mom and Dad on my birthday, and with Nai Nai and Ye Ye the day after. But I don't know if I'll have a party with my friends right away, because Alien-F—Ben was away last week, and I didn't want to have a party if he couldn't come. And then school starts right after my birthday, like it does every year, so everyone will be busy."

"I'm sorry to hear that," my Grandpa Jenkins said. "Maybe you can celebrate with your friends another time."

"Yes," I said, thoughtfully. "That's what Mom said too. We'll see. Mom and Dad are really tired all the time, and busy with the baby, so I don't know."

"Good morning!" A jogger smiled as he ran past.

"Good morning," my grandpa replied.

"Good morning," I said, wishing I had a cap to pat also.

"People are very friendly here," I said, after a moment. "I think maybe it's because they feel guilty, because sneakers and running shorts definitely *don't* count as Sunday best."

"Quite right, Cilla." My grandpa nodded, then glanced at his watch again. "Say, we should probably turn back now. Your grandma wanted me home to run some errands, and you know how she is about being on time."

I raised my eyebrows and nodded understandingly, because I did. My Grandma Jenkins likes things to be "just so."

We headed back across the grassy green field, waving to the people who smiled at us (who were also NOT wearing their Sunday best).

"Thank you, Cilla," my Grandpa Jenkins said as we came up to his house. "This has been a lovely walk."

"Thank you for taking me," I said, giving his arm a hug. "It's a very nice tradition, and I like being in my Sunday best, even if most people don't do it."

"Agreed," he said, opening the front door. "After you, my dear. Do you mind telling your grandma we're back? I think she's in the kitchen."

"Of course not!" I skipped to the kitchen door. "Only she's probably in her office, because it looks like the kitchen light is off." I popped my head in, just to check. "Grandma? Grandma, are you—?"

"SURPRISE!!!!!"

The lights came on.

I couldn't believe my eyes. There were blue streamers all over the ceiling and walls and my mom was holding a cake that said "Happy Birthday, Cilla!" And next to her were Colleen and Alien-Face McGee and Sally and Connor and the Tims and even Sasha. And my grandpa was behind me,

grinning, and there, in the very center of the kitchen, smiling and blowing little party trumpets, were my Grandma Jenkins and, next to her, my *Nai Nai and Ye Ye.*

"Happy birthday!" they shouted.

And then it was all a jumble of noise and hugs and happy birthdays, and Colleen came bouncing up to me and said, "I've had to keep this a secret for FOREVER! If it weren't for Alien-Face reminding me, I would've forgotten and told you!"

And Alien-Face McGee came over and shouted, "Surprise, Silly!"

And Sasha gave me a *hug* and said, "I've missed you, Cilla! Summer break is sooooooooooo long!"

And it was only a few minutes later, when my mom came over and said, "Good surprise?" that the shock began to wear off even a little.

"The best surprise ever!" I threw my arms around her. "Thank you!"

"Thank your grandmas." My mom smiled. "They've been planning this ever since I was in the hospital. And it was your grandpa's idea to have you wear your cheongsam."

So I didn't even have a chance to get over the surprise, or the idea that when they'd been talking in the hospital, they'd been talking about *me*.

I turned wide-eyed to my Grandpa Jenkins.

"You mean," I said, hardly able to believe it, "that the town tradition, strolling in your Sunday best . . ."

"Well . . ." My grandpa looked embarrassed. "It's not exactly true. But your grandmas needed you out of the house, and you needed a reason to wear your dress. I hope you're not too disappointed."

I considered all this slowly. "I'm sad it's not real," I admitted. "But *that*," I said, smiling at my Grandpa Jenkins, "was a *great story*."

"It was." He grinned. "I've learned from the best, after all. Now"—he cleared his throat and turned to talk to everyone else—"let's give the kid her big present, and have some cake."

My dad and my Ye Ye came in from the next

room, and between them, on one of my Grandma Jenkins's plant carts, they wheeled in something big and brown and just my size.

"A desk!" I gasped.

"Made by your Ye Ye," my Grandma Jenkins said proudly.

"Decorated by all of us," my Nai Nai finished.

I ran over to the desk to see, right on the top, six pairs of handprints, pressed on in splashes of green and blue paint.

"A writing desk." My Grandpa Jenkins grinned. "As befits a bestselling author."

I stood there, in my special-occasion cheongsam, smiling so much that my cheeks began to hurt. And just this once, I'll admit that there may be some things writing can't do. Because sometimes, there really are no words.

# PRISCILLA LEE-JENKINS

**We ate chocolate cake and almond cookies,** and Colleen got me a charm bracelet, which is the prize of my jewelry collection. (It's now, in total, a plastic pearl necklace, flower clip-on earrings, a tiara, and the charm bracelet.) And I even *hugged* Alien-Face McGee when I opened his present—a set of manatee-shaped erasers and zoo-animal pencils, which he'd picked out for me all by himself.

After cake and presents, we went out in my Grandma and Grandpa Jenkins's big backyard. My grandma carried The Blob, who had slept through my surprise. My dad and Ye Ye took my new desk outside, and Nai Nai followed behind them carrying a small bucket of paint. Then Colleen and Alien-Face

McGee and all my friends dipped their thumbs in paint, and they put their thumbprints all around the edges of the desk. And then it was my turn.

"We thought you could put your handprints right here," my mom said, pointing to the front drawer, where pens and notebooks would go.

I thought for a moment. I looked at my grandma, and the sleeping Blob. "Actually," I said, "I think I'll save that spot, for now." So I put my handprints on the sides of the desk. And my Grandpa Jenkins took a picture of me doing it, and Colleen and Alien-Face and Sasha and Sally and Connor and the Tims cheered, and I was very happy.

We all washed our hands, and the adults sat on the porch by my grandma's rosebushes while the rest of us played, pushing leaves around in big piles and jumping into them, laughing.

I took a break, though, as the afternoon went on, and went to sit on the grass. I picked a far-off corner and I sat back for a moment, watching my friends run and play, and the adults talking by the house. I thought about Nai Nai and Grandma

Jenkins planning my party, and the idea of Ye Ye making the desk, and Grandpa Jenkins making up a story about traditions, just for me. I thought about how my friends had kept my party a secret because they wanted to surprise me. And I thought about my writing desk, and all those handprints, and the *fourteen* whole thumbprints around its edges, so many that they made a ring around the *entire* desk.

And I looked off for a minute in the other direction, toward the trees of the neighbors' yard and the wooden brown fence just past them.

And then the *most amazing* thing happened.

At first I imagined it was a plane. Then a bird. Then a pterodactyl. But it came closer and closer, falling and falling, and I realized it was a huge cardboard box, wrapped in tinfoil, hurtling toward the ground. I thought it would hit the neighbors' fence with a fiery crash. But at the last second a parachute popped out, and the box landed with just a small thump on the grass in front of me. It wriggled, the cardboard crunched, and a door cut into the side of the box burst open.

"I did it!" a man exclaimed, tumbling out of the box. He saw me, then froze.

"Cilla!" he exclaimed. "Cilla Lee-Jenkins—it's really you!

"Yes, it's me," I said politely, because that's what you do when you meet new people. "Who are you?"

"I'm an inventor," he said with a bow. "I come from the future. My time machine has finally worked!"

"Wow," I said, looking at the cardboard box. "That's impressive."

"Thank you!" He took another small bow. "My calculations, it seems, are a bit off, but it should be no problem at all to reset the machine and take me back to the right date, just about nine years ago. This is very lucky, actually. Now I can be sure to pick a name you'll like. What will it be? Supernova Lilac? Roswitha Hemingway? Eliadora Smith?"

I paused.

"I think," I said after a long, long moment, "I think I'm fine, actually."

The time traveler looked shocked.

"But I thought you wanted a new name. One that's big and exciting and will look great in print."

"I know," I said. "And I did, for a long time. A Priscilla Lee-Jenkins isn't an easy thing to be. But I've gotten used to it. And now that I have, I just don't think I could be anything else."

"Oh," the time traveler said, looking disappointed. "Okay." He ran his fingers through his hair.

"But there are lots of other things you can do," I said gently, "now that you've invented time travel. This is just the beginning. Plus, I think this probably makes you famous. You might want to look into that, actually."

"You may be on to something there." The time traveler wiped his nose, but did look like he felt better. "Well, what about your little sister?" he asked suddenly. "I know you don't like her name, and that you hate it so much you won't even say it. I bet I could go back in time and make sure her name is a good one. Maybe Glimmerella . . ."

"Thank you. But that's okay too," I said firmly. "I think she should get a chance to figure it out for herself. It'll probably be hard," I admitted. "But I'm her older sister, so I'll be there to help."

The time traveler sighed. "I understand. I'm just disappointed. Though," he said, smiling suddenly, "I guess I can do lots of other things, now that I've discovered time travel. Why, I could even go back in time and see a real-life velociraptor!"

"That's the spirit," I cheered.

"Well"—he walked back to his cardboard box and pulled the door open, the foil squeaking as he went—"I'm off. It's been an honor, Priscilla Lee-Jenkins. You're my favorite author. And I've seen you in the future, you know. You signed a book for me, and a copy for my pet flying pig."

"Really?" I asked. "What am I like?"

"You're very famous, of course. All your books are bestsellers, and there's lots of cake."

"I knew it." I smiled. "Thank you."

"And she looks a lot like you. Your little sister."

"She"—I paused—"she does?"

"Why, yes," he said, as if it was the most obvious thing in the world. "When she grows up, she doesn't look like a blob at all. You two have lots of family resemblance."

It was a long moment before I replied.

"Thank you, Mr. Time Traveler," I said, finally. "I'm really glad I got to meet you."

"You too," he said with a smile and another tiny bow. "Well, wish me luck!"

"Good luck!" I waved. "Have fun. And maybe don't get too close to the velociraptors." (He was very nice and had discovered time travel and all, but he somehow didn't seem too bright. At least when it came to common sense.)

"Right," he nodded. Then he gave a small wave and disappeared, with a lot of clunking and shuffling, back into the box. The door swung shut

behind him and the box rose with a wobble, first slowly, then faster and faster, back up, up, up into the sky. And then it was gone.

**"What are you doing, sweetie?"** My mom and dad had come across the yard—my mom holding The Blob, who was still asleep—and were standing next to me, trying to see what I was looking at off in the distance.

"Oh, nothing," I replied. "Just imagining some things that needed to be taken care of. For me"—I put an arm around my mom's waist, and rested my head on her still-kind-of-big stomach—"and . . ." I stopped and looked up at The Blob.

I looked at her scrunched-up face, and I thought about the name my parents had given her, the name I never said, the name I thought was so terrible I wouldn't even write it down.

"And," I said, "for Gwendolyn."

I have to admit—it didn't sound as bad as I'd thought it would.

"Silly," my mom teased, putting an arm around me.

"Yes," I said, taking my dad's hand too. "But only sometimes."

And together, we all walked back to the noise of the party, with the bright, bright orange of the setting sun in the sky behind us. And we all lived happily ever after, Lee and Jenkins alike.

The End

# EPILOGUE: PLOT TWIST

## Ha! I tricked you!

Tricking your reader is called a Plot Twist, and LOTS of bestselling novels have them. So I thought it would be a good idea to end my book with one too.

Also, while happily-ever-afters are okay for fairy tales, I don't think they work for real life. Can you imagine how boring that would be? I mean, sure, I like it when things are happy, but when *everything* is perfect there's very little room for drama.

Or car chases.

The Plot Twist is that my story isn't over at all. There are so many good stories left, like how, a few weeks later, when she was bigger and awake and a bit less breakable, I got to help Gwendolyn dip her hands in paint and put her handprints on the drawer of my writing desk, right at the front. She did a great job, and I was a very careful helper (though some paint may have gotten on the floor. And the wall. Also my mom.).

And to top everything off, the day after my surprise birthday party, there WAS a car chase. It was on the way home from my Grandma and Grandpa Jenkins's house. I think it was an evil villain, out to steal Gwendolyn (who looked GREAT in the excellent outfit I'd chosen for her, as always). Or maybe it was a bank robber who thought our car was filled with money and jewels instead of birthday presents and a (very) smelly diaper. My dad says it was just my Grandpa Jenkins, who doesn't know the shortcut to our house, and had to follow our car in his because we couldn't fit Gwendolyn's stroller in with my new desk. But I kept watch the whole time. Just to be safe—like a responsible Big

Sister. And when we turned corners, I yelled, "Faster, Dad, he's gaining on us!" and "Lose him at the light!" which added EXCELLENT excitement to the ride home, so it was definitely worth the new gray hairs my dad says I gave him. Gwendolyn clearly thought it was fun too, because every time I yelled she also wanted to yell. And she was right to be happy—it made our story perfect.

Because you can't get much better than a car chase.


**Gwendolyn's getting bigger and is growing even** more hair (which isn't fair). But she also smiles when she sees me and giggles when I blow air on her toes, which I like. And even though it'll be a while before she can really and truly make up stories with me, I've discovered that making up stories about her is *a lot* of fun. So far she's been an earthworm, a slug, a puppy, and a troll. Tomorrow, I'm going to make up a story where she goes to the moon, and my mom's even said that I can push Gwendolyn's stroller while I pretend that we're astronauts, as long as I don't let go and promise not to run. So, as you can see, Gwendolyn is *much* more exciting now than she was as a blob in my mom's stomach.

And even though it will be a looooong time before she can read (though hopefully she'll learn a bit faster than I did), that hasn't stopped me from reading to *her*. In fact, just yesterday I started reading Gwendolyn what I hope will be her favorite book someday—this one.

I could only read a little before she started trying to roll away. But she wanted to eat my book, which I think means she likes it. And I know she'll appreciate it A LOT later on, when she can read my life story, and hear about her family, and learn important lessons from my experiences. (Such as, Choco-Rex cereal is VERY disappointing, and NOT what the commercials say it is. The marshmallows don't look ANYTHING like dinosaurs, and they just make the milk a gross, funny-tasting brown color.)

Which means that I'll have a big influence on my little sister. She'll grow up hearing my stories, after all.

I'm starting to see the problem with writing your life's story between the ages of eight and a half and nine. There are just so many more exciting things that keep happening to me—tales of wonder and Struggles, cheese and stegosauruses, imaginary safaris with Colleen (we're going on one next week—there will be polar bears), playing gnomes with Mrs. Tibbs, and of course, drama. Which sells.

And, to add to all this, my Nai Nai and Ye Ye have promised to get me another writing notebook once this one is all used up, because I'm such a good Big Sister, and because even though my first book wasn't done in time for me to become world famous before Gwendolyn was born, I'm still destined for literary greatness, and need to practice for the day when I'll be a bestselling author.

So it really doesn't matter that this is the very last page in the journal my Grandma and Grandpa Jenkins gave me. My book is over, but my writing isn't. Which means that I—Priscilla Lee-Jenkins, future author extraordinaire—will be here again soon, at the special writing desk made just for me, starting at a brand-new Chapter One.

And that, for now, really is The End.

# GLOSSARY:
# CILLA'S GUIDE TO LIFE
# AND LITERARY TERMS

**Ay yah:**

A Chinese way of saying "Wow!" or "Goodness!" or "Oh no!" or "Ooooooh!" or pretty much anything else.

**Best Behavior:**

What you have to be on when you're with lots of adults. Just say "thank you" a lot, and throw in some "pleases" while you're at it. Adults are pretty easy to impress.

**Bestseller:**

This is a book that sells A LOT. When this happens, I'll request covers in all my favorite colors—purple, green, yellow, and chartreuse. Also, maybe one will have a dragon on the cover. But they'll DEFINITELY all have my picture on the back, and will say "From the bestselling author Priscilla Lee-Jenkins," and I'll be very famous. Also rich. And I'll buy a lot of cake with my money but I'll be sure to share it (and to eat it with lots of ice cream). Plus I've promised Colleen that I'll buy her a penguin, which seems only fair because she was my first-ever fan.

## Cheongsam:

A Chinese dress that has a high neck with buttons made of silk string tied in loops. Cheongsams are smooth and soft, and mine has designs made with gold thread all over it. When you say it, it sounds like "sheum sang," which means even its name is pretty. So basically, a cheongsam is the most beautiful kind of dress there is.

## Creative License:

What you can take when you're an author. It means that you can change things in your story, like the words people used, or the colors they were wearing, or what kind of pet they had if you want to make a story more interesting. For example, a story about Mrs. Tibbs and her white pet cat isn't very exciting, and you probably wouldn't want to read it. But a story about Mrs. Tibbs and her neon pink triceratops would probably be a bestseller (see *Bestseller*).

## Drama:

Something exciting, which usually involves explosions or fire or dragons. Every story needs drama, which is why every story is better when there's a car chase.

## Escargot:

Snails. These are delicious, no matter what preschoolers say. And it's pronounced "ess car go," which is fun to say.

## Glossary:

This is a glossary. It helps me define my terms. My Grandpa Jenkins says that all serious books have them. And I'm serious about this book being a best-seller (see *Bestseller*), so it seemed like a good idea.

## Golly:
This is the Jenkins way of saying "ay yah" (see *Ay yah*).

## Literal:
This has something to do with taking things at their face value, which means understanding words just by what they mean. For example, when your mom says, "I'm so hungry I could eat a horse," it just means that she's very hungry, not that she's actually going to find a horse and eat it. This was a BIG relief, because I love horses, even though I've never ridden one because they scare me. I'm getting better at literal things, though I still find it a bit confusing (and I still don't think values can have faces).

## Mood:
How a story feels. Another word for this is Atmosphere, and both are very important. Just be careful

that you don't make the Mood of your story too scary (because then you can't sleep, and your mom isn't as sympathetic as she could be when you explain that you're afraid of the bathroom sink because you wanted to write a scary story, so you imagined a monster that lives in the drain, and now you don't want to wash your hands).

## Nai Nai:

This is the Chinese word for "Grandmother." It's pronounced "Nigh Nigh," not "Nee Nee" or "Nay Nay." If my Nai Nai heard you say it that way, she would say, "Ay yah!" (see *Ay yah*).

## Not Acceptable & Not Going to Happen:

These are the parent words for "no."

## Plot Twist:

When you trick your reader. Lots of bestsellers have them, and my story does too, which means it will *definitely* sell the best, and then I'll be famous.

## Suspense:

How you add drama to a story. Suspense in a book is great, but it's less great in real life, because I can get something called Impatient.

## Theme:

Something that happens again and again and again. Like how my dad always tells me to put my hands in my pockets when we're at a store where there are fragile things, because he's worried I'll touch them and break something. This is an unjust theme, actually, because I'm very careful. (Plus, that one time with the lamp in the antique store wasn't my fault, because how could I have known that the little glass flowers would snap off so easily?) *Anyway*, you'll know when something's a theme when your dad says, "Cilla Lee-Jenkins, we've been over this a thousand times!"

## Tzuck Sang:

Bamboo hearts. This is my Nai Nai's favorite food and my favorite food, which is an EXCELLENT thing to have in common with someone (because if you can't bond over food, then what else is there?). And it also has an excellent name. When you say it, it sounds like "jook-sang."

## Wah:

This is the Chinese way of saying "Ta-da!" or "Oh my!" or "Great!" or anything else "ay yah" doesn't cover.

## Ye Ye:

This is the Chinese word for "Grandfather." It's pronounced "Yeh Yeh," not "Yee Yee" or "Yay Yay." If my Ye Ye heard you say it that way, he would refer you to my Nai Nai (see *Nai Nai*), who would say, "Ay yah!" (see *Ay yah*). (This glossary business is very confusing.)

## Young Lady:

What you are when you're in trouble.

# ACKNOWLEDGMENTS

**There are so many people who helped make this** book possible.

Thank you first to my family: my mom and dad, who have believed in me every step of the way; Grandmom and Bobby; Catherine, who gave Cilla her full name, and Sarah, who told me unequivocally that I *had* to finish this book; Charles and Henry; Ethan, Dan, Courtney, and Aysun; Auntie Esther and Uncle Paul, who support me with their faith and enthusiasm; Jenn, Yvonne, Kimmy, Mike, Paul, Jeff, Jeremy, Rachel, Ellie, Emmett, and Noah; and Nai Nai, Ye Ye, Eh-Pah, and Dede, who I will never stop missing.

A huge thank-you to Dan Lazar, who started me on this publishing journey and has been an enthusiastic advocate and vital source of support every step of the way. Thank you to Connie Hsu for your brilliant and creative eye, and for pushing me to never shy away from complexity and hard, true moments. You've made every step of this process a joy, and taught me so much about writing along the way. Cilla wouldn't be Cilla without you!

Thank you, too, to the teams at the Writers House and Roaring Brook: to Torie for fielding all my questions, to Megan for your insights and excitement about the book, to Andrew Arnold for a beautiful book design, and to all the publicity and marketing teams at Roaring Brook for your enthusiasm and support.

This book wouldn't be complete without the beautiful artwork of Dana Wulfekotte. Thank you for bringing Cilla and her family to life, for your commitment to representation, for your patience with my endless suggestions, for the care and detail in every image and face you so beautifully sketch, and, of course, for the rainbow unicorn.

Thank you to my childhood friends: Colleen, Annalee, Courtney, Ben, Laura H., Laura S., Arthur, Patrick from Gladstone, Kelly from Michigan, and the Brame, Mulhall, and Scott families. I can think of no greater gift for Cilla than friends and communities like you.

Thank you to the teachers and role models whose names and stories also fill this book: Ms. Stroud, Ms. Gatlin, Ms. Jill, Ms. Garfield, Ms. Shear, Mr. Winch, Lynn Bloom, Lynn Love, Maria, Morag, and Ms. Davies.

Thank you to my community at UMass Boston for

your unflagging support even when my career goals took a slight turn. Thank you, Cheryl, Renata, Erin, Sarah, Hugh, Dan, Matt, Sam, and Susan T., and the students in my Children's Writing Workshop, who energize and inspire me.

Thank you to the Writers' Room of Boston: Debka, Alexander, Camille, Kate, and everyone else at WROB, you truly changed my life and made Boston home.

Thank you to my friends, who have cheered me on from both sides of the Atlantic: Olivia, Valerie, Emily Jaeger, Perri, Lauren, Emily Rockett, Erica, Zoe, Connor, Becky, and Rachel.

And finally, to the best of friends, Yanie, Hannah, and Ashley. I, and this book, would be nothing without you. You are my Colleens and Alien-Faces, my Ms. Lynns and Ms. Blooms; you infuse my book with your love and belief. Thank you, Yanie, for the writing talks that set me on my way; Hannah, for being my first-ever editor; and Ashley, for giving me the idea in the first place.